# INFLUX

AN EVE OF LIGHT STORY

HARAMBEE K. GREY-SUN

HYPERVERSE BOOKS, LLC

Cover design by The Cover Collection.

Print ISBN-13: 978-1-64044-020-3

Ebook ISBN-13: 978-1-64044-019-7

Published by HyperVerse Books, LLC

www.hyperversebooks.com


Crossing genres without apologies.

ONE

Henri had never seen the communal laundry room so full, not even on Sunday evenings.

On those worldly occasions, mindless rituals were performed to ensure clean clothing for the week ahead. The slight throbbing at his temples served as a reminder of an ill-spent Friday evening as he wondered what kind of cleansing ritual he and his neighbors had been herded together for on this Saturday morn.

The condo association's joyless team had spread out at sunrise, going door to door, knocking on all one hundred and fifty to extend a "good morning" to any who were unsure and to encourage all—roommates, children, overnight guests—to meet in the facilities building by ten thirty. Pets were to be left behind. And under no circumstances should anyone make any attempt to leave the premises of the condominium complex.

Following instructions with a care for urgency but not much thought, Henri pulled on some old khaki shorts and a slightly cleaner T-shirt than the one he'd slept in. He slid his calloused feet into his Birkenstocks and locked his apartment's front door behind him.

Having made space for themselves in the center of the laundry room, each member of the condo board wielded a cordless mic, a necessary tool for crowd control. Small speakers had been arranged at strategic points around the room. Henri wondered whether they'd excite or calm, hoping for the latter. He figured the ideas, needs, and desires among his neighbors on how to spend a Saturday morning were varied, but none would have landed on spending the time in cramped, noisy laundry room.

He'd gotten himself as close to the center as possible. Forget the speakers—he wanted no electronic interpretation, preferring to be close enough to read these people's lips if necessary.

Everyone who was coming to the room was there by ten. Those wise enough to arrive at least an hour early got the cushioned folding chairs; others sat on the cold steel chairs or made themselves comfortable on the floor. More than a few made do by hoisting themselves up onto the folding tables or the machines making up the rows of back-to-back washers and dryers. The room seemed to share the circumference of a high school's gymnasium—a rich kid's high school. The property's building designers must've foreseen a time when everyone might need to do their laundry on the same day. Separate from and centered amid the condo buildings, it provided the best possible meeting room in the absence of a formal one.

Even with so many people making generous contributions to the roar of casual conversations and speculations, much of the noise fell to a near hush when Jessie, the association manager, stood up, clutching a cordless microphone. A big-boned six-foot-three woman with a big blonde pompadour, she had a penchant for platform heels, tight jeans, revealing blouses, and tomato-red lipstick. She rarely had a problem drawing attention without saying a word—or maybe it was just Henri's attention. Maybe the surrounding sounds of the natural world flushed away whenever his eyes landed on her. He couldn't turn away, not even for a glance, as she raised the mic, bringing it to rest just inches from those plump red lips.

"As you've all heard in the news," Jessie said, "the local military units are staging war games all this week. I was informed late last night that activities will be passing through this area starting around noon and continuing on until sundown. We were asked to gather you all here. Barricades and checkpoints have been set up so that any of your neighbors or family members who were off-site will be prevented from returning to the grounds until all this is finished. We will be providing sandwiches, chips, and beverages in the hall. I trust you all know where the restrooms are."

She waved her arms in a flourish, as if to indicate they were practically in a forest of restrooms, before she retook her seat and leaned to whisper something to the salt-and-pepper-haired man next to her. Everyone else was left to stand and stretch, sit quietly, or talk among themselves. Some mumbled that they wished they'd brought books or tablets; others bowed their heads, devoting themselves to their smartphones.

Henri didn't worship his phone, and he wasn't in the mood for conversing with anyone near him. Not that he was particularly asocial. He'd met and liked many of his closest neighbors, all of them in their thirties or forties and all of them committed bachelors, content bachelorettes, or cheerful divorcees who'd vowed to never walk down the aisle again. It was a good group; they often had interesting discussions in more relaxed environments. But Henri had nothing except questions today, the same questions the people around him kept asking one another.

He'd no desire to contribute to the echo chamber.

He hopped off the dryer and wound his way through the maze of machines, heading toward the association manager.

Jessie had already left her seat and was standing near the entry to the hallway, surrounded by the other condo board members, all of them speaking in hushed tones. Each appeared worried about something. Henri couldn't tell what. When their eyes fell on him, their lips stopped moving. One or two glared. Henri slowed but continued his approach.

"Yes?" The man with salt-and-pepper hair addressed Henri when he breached the gathering's comfort zone. Henri had never met him but recognized him as the guy who barked orders at the "green guys"—the folks in green jumpsuits whose jobs apparently entailed nothing other than tending to the property's lawn and smoking another sort of grass while leaning against residents' cars. No one ever referred to them as "maintenance" with a straight face.

Henri ran his eyes over all of them before responding, hoping to engage with someone else. "I, uh, just wanted to ask what's going on."

"Jessie already went over all that." Gruff seemed to be Salt-and-Pepper's consistent tone, indoors and out.

"But I work six days a week," Henri said, deepening his own voice. "Saturday is pretty much the only day I have to run errands, and I have a lot of them."

"You can run them tonight."

Henri's brow furrowed. "A lot of places I need to go to

will be closed by then." He may not have immediately appeared so to the man with salt-and-pepper hair, or to anyone else, but Henri wasn't easily intimidated. A man in his line of work couldn't afford to be.

Salt-and-Pepper perhaps felt the same. He stepped closer, narrowing his eyes as he asked, "What's your name, son?" Six inches taller than Henri, the man perhaps hoped that closing the distance and raising his chin might help do what words alone weren't doing—chasing Henri away. "Just where do you need to go so badly?"

Henri kept his jaw firm, but he wanted to chuckle. Every sentence out of the man's mouth was punctuated with a growl, as if he were a guard dog ready to sink his teeth into a trespasser.

But Henri knew all bark and no bite when he heard it. He'd dealt with twelve-year-olds in the mall who were legitimately tougher than this codger.

"Relax, Toby." Jessie finally stepped forward. "This is Mr. Henri Benoit."

"Ben-*wah*?" Toby tilted his head slightly. "What the hell—?"

"It's French," Henri volunteered.

Toby looked positively disgusted. "A Frenchie, huh? Same breed of the folks who refuse to take our side against overseas terrorists."

It could've been Henri's complete lack of an accent—and thus a lack of any warning—that so perturbed Toby, or maybe it was because the barker looked almost old enough to vividly remember World War II as well as some more recent global disagreements.

Both thoughts occurred to Henri as he allowed himself a smirk. "Actually, I was born in Quebec."

Seeing Toby's fingers twitch, he promoted his smirk to a

wry smile, hoping to help the codger complete the process of making fists. Henri was as easygoing as any stereotype from north of the border, but he was raised in the American Midwest. He didn't mind pushing buttons, particularly those marked "Go" or "Play."

"You a *stick-and-puck* fan, Toby?"

Toby started forward, his arms raising to swing, but Jessie was quicker, reaching and grabbing the man's shoulder, staying off a punch.

"Mr. *Benoit*," she said, "is one of our *least* troublesome residents." Jessie gazed at Henri rather than Toby as she spoke.

*Point taken*, Henri thought. He relaxed his shoulders and took a conciliatory step backward.

Toby stood his ground but relaxed, giving Jessie permission to remove her hands. She flattened one against her stomach and laid the other hand on her hip—a stance meant to draw attention, making whatever she had to say next easier to absorb.

"Henri," she said in a honeyed tone, "we are as distressed about this situation as you. The military gave us very little warning and no options. Just be glad you're inside a big safe building like this. It was built to withstand tornados, fires, and floods—anything gruesome—and we have plenty of food and access to working restrooms. Those left off the property, heaven knows where the gatekeepers will herd them."

Henri frowned. "If they're at the front gates, why can't they just be put in here with the rest of us?"

"Not the gates to the parking lot." Melinda, another board member, approached. "The *checkpoints*. The roads have been blocked off for miles. Anyone who was on the streets an hour ago isn't on them now." The fifty-something woman apparently hadn't had time for hairstyling, let alone makeup. Her worry lines were apparent, and shifting.

"So, again," Jessie said, "you're lucky. Being here in a sturdy building ready to withstand the worst of what nature and man can throw at it." She attempted a smile but lacked the conviction to make it work. Henri knew she had nothing to smile about. None of them did.

"Why don't you go grab a soda and relax?" Melinda gestured toward the archway leading to the nearest hallway.

Henri got it. The folks in charge of the inside had said all they were going to say to him, so he should go get lost already. He wasn't hungry, but with a sigh, he decided to check out what the hallway spread had to offer.

In his estimation, it wasn't half bad. Quite a few agreed. There seemed to be enough people crowding the long table to form two baseball teams, all of them mixing chatter about the layout and their predicament.

He weaved through the throng, figuring someone must have hired a caterer, the sort of professional who worked early and at a moment's notice. Had to be pricey—and the money would undoubtedly come out of the condo fees, which would undoubtedly double next month.

Peering through the spaces between shuffling bodies, he catalogued at least a dozen different types of sandwiches— all sorts of meats and breads—and six different salty snacks, eight varieties of canned beverages, including tea and soda, and just one generic brand of bottled water. A smaller crowd frequented a separate table featuring the yin-yang of a large vegetable platter and a large cookie platter. Whoever was in charge of this setup sure wanted to make people forget about the outside world for a while. He snatched up two peanut butter cookies and pulled himself away from the masses as he started down the hall, keeping close to the outermost brick wall as best he could.

Brightened by some natural light and more generous portions of the fluorescent sort emanating from the recessed fixtures above, the brick and linoleum hallway was roughly ten to twelve feet wide, allowing plenty of room for the two-way traffic of passersby pushing laundry carts or lugging multiple duffels stuffed with dirty clothes. The four hallways surrounding the rectangle of the laundry room all joined at right angles, making for one rectangular passageway.

Despite Jessie's dramatic hand-waving earlier, Henri and all the other residents knew restrooms were only located in the two shorter hallways of the rectangle. The longer hallways' walls were punctuated by utility closets and other small rooms in addition to doors, some leading to the outside, and circular windows—evenly spaced and alternating between six and ten feet high—each of them just slightly larger than a man's head.

As he strolled, glancing through what may as well have been portholes, Henri could see how this building was a much safer environment than the six surrounding condo buildings. Each apartment contained large patio doors made almost completely of glass.

Turning a corner into a shorter hallway, he heard a deep rumble, a nearby thunderclap perhaps. The war games must have started. Though the windows were small, instinct pushed him to hurry away from the nearest one as others in the hall also kept their distance. He shoved the remainder of his second cookie into his mouth before pushing into the men's room.

Fifteen minutes later, after relieving himself and examining the bags under his eyes, he reentered the hall feeling lighter in the stomach, a little lighter in the head, but no more fully awake.

He didn't know what had possessed him to stay out until last call. He'd known he'd have to get up early. He'd known he had errands to run today. If only he'd set his alarm an hour earlier, he could've gotten a head start. But, then, he wouldn't be *here*. He'd be *out there*, among the barred.

He heard another rumble, longer and deeper than the one previous. Much longer. It seemed to vibrate the entire building, deepening the volume of chatter from those clogging the hall. Most were wise enough to stay away from the windows; many hustled for the doors leading to the laundry area. Henri wondered whether the sound resulted from an explosion or just an irresistible vehicle meeting some immovable object. Whatever it was, the walls and floor continued to tremble, forcing Henri to make an extra effort to maintain his balance.

As he rounded a corner, passing into the next long hall, another peal struck, this one unmistakably shaking the building, stirring even more loiterers to find their way back to the relative safety of the washers and dryers. Good sense dictated that Henri follow—but he hesitated.

He resented being penned up like this. He hated the fact it was interfering with his day of catch-up. He didn't appreciate the lack of a day-before heads-up, just enough of a warning giving him the opportunity to hole up in a motel for the night, to not have to deal with any of this. But here he was—in the dark . . . cut off from his day-to-day reality . . . nostrils tickled by insipid aromas.

Wafting into the hall were the sweet smells of laundry detergent competing with the musk of body odor, the perspiration—Henri figured—an unfortunate result of the dryers' heat. The vents weren't working as well as they should've been. No surprise to him. What was going his or any other resident's way today?

Another rumble—disrupting the mild tremoring of the hall—forced him to move as the walls and floor settled into a rhythm of trembling faster than before. Standing still was an impossibility. Yet, he didn't stumble toward the nearest laundry room door. A heady mix of spite and curiosity drew him to the closest window.

He placed his palms flat against the wall's surface on either side of the glass circle to help maintain his footing. The wall hummed his skin as he peered outside, expecting to see at least one tank. Instead he just saw the natural outdoors, all of it passing by as if he were sitting on a train that had just left the station.

Buildings, trees, cars, and other vehicles . . . Nothing remained in sight long enough for him to describe in significant detail. Yet, after a moment, he thought he saw the same vehicles, trees, and other landmarks passing in the same order; and after another moment, the same. It seemed as if the building were spinning on an axis.

Or maybe he was just dizzy.

He pushed himself away from the window and turned around, his arms raised to prevent him from tumbling down. A smattering of other people still milled about, perusing the edible offerings while also trying to maintain their footing. None were stupid enough to go anywhere near the windows, let alone try to gaze through one.

Continuing to put distance between himself and it, Henri turned, tossing a glance back at the window. It was too small and he was now too far away to make out anything other than rapidly changing shades of light. Nothing to draw anyone's attention. No different than watching the effects of sunlight battling with cloud cover, either side winning at any given moment.

No one other than he seemed to give a care about the windows or what was happening beyond them. And he'd no desire to be the crazy guy running up to people, tapping them on the shoulder to ask if they thought the building was moving. He certainly wouldn't think of asking anyone to take the risk of peering out of one of the windows themselves. What he'd seen could just be the late onset of a hangover, its effects stirred by an abundance of natural light.

Another thunderclap, followed by a long, low rumble throughout the hall—like a just-out-of-sight dump truck repeatedly and haphazardly raising and lowering capacity-filled steel dumpsters. It was enough to push the remaining laggards back into the laundry room where they undoubtedly hoped the harsh sounds wouldn't reach them.

As the lights flickered, Henri made his way to the beverage table and grabbed two bottles of water. He downed one in several gulps, hoping it would help detox him, wake him up, steady his balance—*something*.

He tossed the empty water bottle into the recycling bin and reentered the big room, anxious to see how the others were occupying their time. Complacently, it seemed. And with good reason.

The floor wasn't trembling. The lighting was fine. The walls were thick enough to keep the outdoor noises at bay. Some folks had been wise enough to bring their laundry; others had brought decks of cards to play poker, solitaire, or whatever else. Even if the walls had been thinner, the multitudes of conversations and whirring machines were more than a match for the thunderclaps.

"Hey, Henri, you want in?"

To his left, his friend and two-doors-down neighbor

Dave leaned against a dryer and pointed down toward a mini-cooler. Of course some wise guy would sneak alcohol in here. And of course Dave would be so wise.

Henri lazily lifted his hand, showing off the bottled water.

Dave raised an eyebrow. "You sure?" He lifted the lid of the cooler with his scuffed sneaker, just enough to show off a few cans of beer and juice-box-size white wines.

Henri shook his head then asked, "Have you been out in the hall? Did you look outside of the window?"

"Hell no"—Dave jerked back his sneaker, letting the cooler lid clap shut—"why would I? This place isn't as safe as Jessie and her microphone posse say it is. Not a lot of windows out there, but what *is* there isn't bulletproof. Even the fake bullets the soldiers are using out there could sail right on through. I ran to grab a couple'a sandwiches and chips, but I ain't even going to attempt to catch a piece of the action."

*Sensible,* Henri thought—much more so than trying to convince Dave to go back and take a little peek.

He took several gulps from the water bottle then, groaning, plopped down opposite Dave.

As Henri leaned his back against a washer in midcycle, Dave asked, "What the hell's wrong with you?"

"Think I might be sick."

"Overdid it last night, huh?" Annabelle, a four-doors-down neighbor, approached with a sly smile on her lips, examining Henri, her eyelids tightening as she perhaps conjured up a synopsis of his night and began wondering whether she should give voice to her speculations.

She raised her chin, peered down at him over the length of her chiseled nose, and spoke with her tongue clinging close to the roof of her mouth. "Moderation, moderation,

moderation . . ." She turned to Dave. "I learned the hard way. Last time I tied one on, I woke up in a very unfamiliar neighborhood—to say nothing of the bed . . . if one could even charitably call a bunch of shredded clothing a 'bed.'"

Henri gaped at her.

She cleared her throat and said, "I hooked up with a fashion designer, who had a fetish for shredding clothes that were out of style—if you must know."

Henri started to say he didn't need to know and that, in fact, no one would have needed to know if she hadn't brought it up. Dave was quicker to speak.

"Happened to me more than once," he said. "Not *that* scenario—but similar."

"What?" Henri muttered. "Did you wake up on a bed of rolled-up sweaty socks?"

"Heh. Funny—but, no. No regrets about where I woke up or with whom—or even when they went *ghost,* and I, whether I liked it or not, left the premises without a goodbye or kiss. But I will say I regret some of the dustups I've gotten into, arguing over . . . Well, hell, who remembers afterwards? But this scar here"—he quickly raised his left fist toward an unflinching Annabelle—"there on my knuckle? The one that looks like a bite mark? That's one hell of a reminder not to get drunk in certain locales. A lesson that one needs to know how to read environments, even if the vision's a bit blurry."

Henri felt as if he were reading a picture book translating itself into braille with each turn of the page. Images slowly disintegrating into colored points and moving dots convinced his eyes to not even try as a performance of needlepoint picked up pace within his cranium.

"What were you drinking?" Annabelle asked Dave.

"Just beer," he said.

"Bottled? I heard that the government is mandating that all bottled alcoholic beverages distributed to bars and restaurants have a . . . *certain* ingredient, unnamed and unlisted anywhere. And some manufacturers put in too much."

"*Certain* ingredient?"

"Maybe just one or maybe a few that react well together. Net says it's some kind of seeds that're mashed up until they're powders; no scent, no taste, and easily mixed with certain alcoholic beverages. Whatever—they're supposed to make drinkers more susceptible to believing what's being transmitted over the airwaves. *Subliminals* in the television and music that's always playing in these places. Sports shows, news shows, only certain genres of music . . ."

"Subliminals, huh? Like, '*Hey! Your drink is really good, right? Get another!*'"

"More like vital info they want us to know but not panic about."

"Don't drink and drive? Don't drink and hook up?"

Annabelle nodded. "I think that's what they're building toward."

"Well"—Dave scratched his ear—"I don't know about all that . . . but I do know that mixed drinks are where they really get you these days. That's why I avoid them."

"Something in the sweeteners?"

"Something in the ice cubes. When they melt—"

Henri couldn't bear any more. His waking hours had been excruciating enough. While Dave and Annabelle delved deeper into conspiracy theories, he let his eyelids provide him comfort. It was going to be a long day. He hoped to take a long nap. The vibrating machine at his back and the attendant sounds of sloshing likely wouldn't allow him to rest for too long, not after he'd consumed so much water. But a couple of moments of shut-eye would do nicely.

He only hoped, while in whatever slumber he fell into, he didn't wet himself.

Though . . . in the long run . . . *What did it really matter?*

What further humiliation mattered, what did *anything* matter if one was prevented from achieving a dream? Realizing a fantasy? Henri used to wonder how many failures one had to withstand before understanding why they'd been put on Earth in the first place, before truly comprehending what role they were destined to play. Now he felt the heaviness of his bladder and grimly wondered how many humiliations one deserved after realizing their destiny would be forever out of their reach.

His humiliations in life had been many, but none as great as the day he washed out of training camp for the Peacemakers—the Heartland Security Agency's own special forces.

Armed men and women tasked with taking to the field in the name of the Agency's mission of preserving families, protecting children, and promoting safe and happy communities—in short, securing America's heartland and, thus, ensuring its future. It hadn't quite been a lifelong dream, but it had been a dream injected into his young adult life like a vaccination, a dream that necessarily changed his perception of the world and his place in it.

As late as high school, he'd had no strong ambitions, no noble aspirations. He'd graduated with no claim other than being a mediocre varsity wrestler whose arm was out of whack owing to him going through multiple seasons acting as if his body was more flexible than it really was. No counselor had to push or prod, nor even condescend; he was happy to attend the local trade school.

The future was blue and white—a blue sky and a few puffy white clouds. The majority of people who worked would be blue-collar workers, with a few clusters of white collars—or so the talking heads he'd enjoyed listening to on cable news and the radio had said. At the rate technology was progressing, many folks at all levels would be displaced. But no matter what robots or other automations might come, there would always be a need for humans to work the details of law enforcement, public utilities, and a wide variety of specialized care. Recession-proof occupations. He threw in his lot with the electricians.

Once President Sullivan was offed, however, Henri yearned for something more.

The sturdiness of his profession was put to the test when, in the wake of the president's assassination, the country plunged into a recession. The talking heads' prophecy had proven true, and he was grateful to be able to keep working, keep earning, while he worked just as meticulously on his HSA application and awoke each morning with anticipation.

When his phone finally buzzed, he'd been doing the wiring on a home security system for a financial adviser who'd been afraid some of the born-swarthy and newly indigent might pay him a visit at some inconvenient hour. Taking the call, Henri was mostly successful in tuning out the man's vociferous fretting about a vulnerable "high-end property." When he hung up the phone, his back was a little straighter; his chest, broader; his heart pumped the blood of a New American in the making.

In two weeks, he relocated, setting up shop in a decent

enough motel—its decency based on its proximity to a police station.

He passed the tests: drugs, vision, hearing, written, even the polygraph. The interviews had been nerve-racking—but he made it through the gauntlet. Of course, his shoulder had been noticed. The knob of skin on his shoulder signified a bone out of place, hinted at a man out of place . . . But in the end, the worries were erased, or at least covered with some optimism that he might have qualities that would allow him to overcome a minor physical deficiency.

He couldn't get into the evaluators' minds, but *he* had optimism. Enough for an army. He knew he could serve his country. He was certain he'd the *stuff* that could easily be remade into the type of being necessary to secure the Heartland.

But the actual training wiped him out.

He wouldn't accept failure. He rejected shame. Rather than go back to being an electrician working for home-owners and companies, no matter how well paying, he searched for every job he could find that called for a more hands-on type of security. Mall security was as good as he could get in the short term—but it was only temporary.

While honing his mind and body, he was constantly on the search for a more appropriate job, a position that would allow him to prove himself in the public eye if and when necessary. He held out hope the HSA would call him back, allow him to try again. He had impressed some of his trainers with his determination. And every other Monday he emailed the recruiting department to let them know he was still interested. But even if that call never came, the way that certain segments of American society behaved when out of work, he was certain he'd have his chance to do his part to secure the Heartland, even if he had to act alone.

"*Excuse* me."

The high-pitched voice was like something slippery wriggling down his ear canals. Henri's eyelids fluttered apart, allowing a bleary view of someone's baggy knees.

"Do you *mind?*"

Henri lifted his chin and saw an older, bespectacled man, his hands planted firmly on his hips as he glared down at him.

"*I'm* trying to make the best of my time here. And *you're* in my way."

Henri then realized what he was going on about. "Oh. Uh. Sorry." He pushed himself up to his feet and quickly stepped aside, several sudden movements that made him realize his insides were ready for a flush.

He made a beeline for the nearest doorway.

He didn't so much as even glance at any of the windows as he trotted toward the restrooms. He pushed his way through the men's room door, passed the stalls in brief wonderment that they were empty, then did his business at the first urinal he reached.

Gazing into the mirror as he washed his hands, he noticed the bags and redness had mostly disappeared. Maybe when he entered the hall this time he'd see a scene completely different from when he'd last exited the restroom.

A *burbling* came from one of the stalls behind him. Disturbed water. He figured there must've been someone inside it after all. He then heard similar *urbling* sounds coming from all the stalls.

All of them couldn't have been occupied. He pivoted, approached the nearest, and crouched down to peer under the door. No feet, but the bubbling sound increased, as if the toilets were boiling pots on a stove.

He'd heard this sound before, limited to one toilet, in his old apartment. Living on the ground floor of a six-story building underneath folks who never gave a damn about flushing paper towels, tampons, cat litter . . . It was the reason he'd moved out.

The old image in his mind was suddenly complemented by the sight of steaming brown liquid cascading from the toilet bowls onto the floor, like some rapidly melting solid too big to be contained. Henri sprang up, backpedaling before turning to bolt when he realized the water wasn't creeping—it was *running*.

He was a few steps into the hall when a thickening haze engulfed him—a fragrant and almost intoxicating mist. He momentarily wondered if the green guys had been allowed to live it up while he was in the restroom.

But the haze didn't smell of weed; it had a sweeter, woodsier aroma. Nor did he see the green guys, nor anyone else. A disappointment, as he would've steered them directly to the restroom. The provocative brume, though, seemed to push and pull him in its drift until he found himself near another window.

Its frame had changed to an irregular almond shape, lopsided. The glass had taken on a light brownish yellow tint. Henri tilted his head, squinting, as he peered through and watched the outdoors passing by as if he were inside a bullet train, one running a track configured like a pretzel.

In less than a minute's time, he turned away from the window, queasy and stumbling about like a child playing pin-the-tail. It wasn't just what he felt inside. There was something on the floor, something that coated the linoleum and made Henri momentarily feel as if he were in an old movie theater after a long day of double features.

He couldn't quite make it out through the haze, but

whatever was on the floor *glistened*. The more he tried to get a clearer picture while stumbling, the more the glistening gave him the impression of sunlight dancing on rippling, murky water. The fragrant haze was nauseating. He figured his mind had been taunted into playing tricks.

He forced himself to stop moving and stand still, back straightened. Eyes closed and breath held, he tried to enforce a sense of balance.

But he swayed. He stepped a little to the left. A little to the right. A little every which way as the stench from the restroom steadily found its way through the haze, into his nostrils.

On the verge of contributing his own waste to the floor, Henri's eyes jerked open as he forced himself in a quicker pace toward the general direction of the laundry area.

But a straight route to anything eluded him.

The haze had become murkier. The corridor, darker. The passage seemed much wider than before—though he figured he'd just been stumbling about in an imperfect circle. A theory confirmed, he thought, when his shoulder grazed a wall.

Instinctively he pressed his hands to it, flattening his palms as they slid for several inches across the oleaginous surface. He forced a greater area of his body against the wall. He had to find balance—and he wasn't sure how much of the slipperiness was a result of his own sweat. His clothes were damp with perspiration, though he didn't feel all that warm. *Just how much did I drink last night?* Was this some kind of relapse?

Or were one of his neighbors' conspiracy theories correct? Last night, had there been something in his drink other than the expected ingredients of a normal lager?

The puckered wall seemed to buckle and expand with

the unsteady rhythm of a broken bellows. The volleying sensations in his legs were almost a match. Weak knees at one moment; assured tendons at the next. He wondered if he was on the verge of collapse.

He couldn't see more than a foot in front of him. In any direction. He listened for others—there *had* to be others—but he heard no voices, only sounds . . . Polyphonic . . . Inhuman . . . Almost mechanical. Guttural groans. Distant screams that transitioned to sustained whistles. An omnipresent sizzling.

Were the laundry machines on the fritz? Surely, he would've heard his more vociferous neighbors clamoring about that. Surely, at this point, he should've heard his neighbors clamoring about *something*.

He called out, hoping for a response, only to hear more of the same mechanical sounds and a sampling of some new: a *grinding* threaded with a motor's purr; the shrill Morse code of malfunctioning smoke detectors; sheets of foil battered by stop-and-go wind gusts.

He wouldn't panic. He wouldn't dart off to be swallowed in the gloom. No matter how far he strayed, he kept coming back to the wall, despite its multiplying number of slick pustules that throbbed at his touch. He *queased* each time, but his repulsions were short-lived. He had to maintain proximity to a steady influence. The wall was his only option. He stuck close—until the wall curved sharply away from him.

Urged by a particularly violent undulation of floor and walls, he stumbled through an opening his eyes hadn't seen and landed on a thick rubbery surface overgrown with short, stiff bristles.

The bristly pad quickly gave way, sending him to tumble down a lengthy tube lined with an abundance of moist flapping membranes until he landed back-down on an unyielding platform with a *plosh*.

Lying faceup on a slush-soft ground that undulated like a waterbed, Henri shouted, intending to release a cry that expressed more pain than he actually felt. Confusion and frustration were the true impetuses. Regardless, his vocals failed to rise above the disconsolate groan permeating the musty air.

He contributed softer grunts to the audible misery while digging his hands deeper into the slush for a firmer surface, heaving himself up to a standing position, all while clenching his teeth, trying not to take in too much of the miasma as he wished away any pain he felt as a temporary inconvenience.

His shirt and shorts were ripped but remained wearable, even if they and much of his skin were covered with a glistening dew that seemed faint orange in the dim light. The somber atmosphere made it difficult to see more than a few feet around him, but that was all it took to notice the broken sign a few paces away.

Upright yet steadily sinking, the sign's markings had faded, but he made out some words, just enough of the popular makeup brand's name, just enough of the address. He knew the words well. The sign was from a mall's kiosk—the mall where he worked as chief security guard.

Aimlessly, he stumbled, glancing about to spot signs from other kiosks, each of them gradually sinking deeper into opaque pools of limited circumference. Their faint letters and designs continued to fade as their edges melted until—suddenly—the entire object dissolved with a frantic sizzle. With each object's dissolution, Henri noticed a shift in the air, a new scent—almost floral—before a return to the foul usual.

Fragments of thoughts darted about his mind. His mouth mimicked, pushing forth grunts and gasps rather than coherent words. His head shook involuntarily until a new sight snagged his attention.

A cluster of bodies, more than half-submerged. They were upright, yet leaning in various positions as they slowly sank into dense pools.

*Mannequins* was his first resounding thought. They had no eyes. They made no sounds. They didn't struggle. Yet something about their facial features seemed a little too detailed. Their dingy attire would not have seemed fashionable under the best circumstances.

As they sizzled from sight in unison, a new odor greeted Henri, as if a perfume kiosk at the mall had collided with the dumpster nearest its food court.

His right knee twitched as he attempted a step backward. The same with his left. His feet weren't moving. Lowering his chin, he saw them submerged.

What had seemed like slush only moments before now had the appearance of a soupy liquid, greenish gray, as firm as it was impenetrable to sight. Henri had the impression of liquid cement as, with a concentrated effort, he managed to lift one foot then the other before quickly moving to find less hostile ground.

His sandals were gone. Even in the poor light, he saw that his throbbing feet appeared badly bruised. The shock was enough to lift both knees and send him running, dodging any obstacles that emerged from the haze in his path. His thoughts raced in a like manner, but one remained settled—if he stayed put, he was going to dissolve, just like the signs. Just like the frozen figures. As it was, his feet tingled, sending shrieks through his lower legs' nervous system with each step.

He had to escape. He hadn't many options for the route.

Noticing the haze to his left assume a different hue, he pushed on in that direction, soon finding himself in a narrow circular tunnel, its walls lined with large, brick-red lumps that slowly pulsed, giving him the impression of a sore throat steadily constricting and expanding.

He slowed his pace to a brisk walk.

The haze was thinner here, gossamer enough for Henri to take fresh note of the glistening dew coating his person. Flecks no bigger than half the size of his fingernails lay scattered about his skin and clothes, held in place by the staunch moisture. He guessed they numbered three to four dozen as he tried to brush them away. None budged. That his hands were just as slick as the rest of him was likely a factor.

The tenacious flecks held his attention as he trudged on. They'd a flame-orange hue, and a metallic sheen, like foil. When the surrounding lumps expanded, the flecks darkened to rust; when the lumps contracted, the hues brightened to amber.

*Call and response,* Henri weakly thought before dismissing the notion.

This—his entire experience—was just a lucid dream. He hadn't woken up after shutting his eyes in the laundry room. He'd fallen into a deep, penetrating sleep only to strike the oil of grotesqueries, dreams painted with pigments that were binding his thoughts to Pandemonium . . .

It was as if he'd fallen asleep while sniffing glue, inhaling *rubber cement* . . . sly fumes . . .

Presently his nostrils caught traces of burning rubber . . . steaming sewage . . . rotting carcasses . . . *sulphur* . . .

The odors changed with each inhalation, the sensory effect of each prolonged due to Henri trying to hold his breath as much as possible. He kept trying, even as the tunnel broadened, opening into a cavernous space—but the new sights elicited gasps. His heart raced as he realized his lucid dream floated upon an appalling theme.

He sloshed his way through a disarray of store signs, carts, heaps of clothing, furniture; the occasional cash register, baby stroller, piece of luggage, unpaired shoe; a wide variety of unrecognizable objects; hunks of metal, panes of cracked glass, and other irregular shapes he had to imagine were once part of an escalator, department store display case, or something else he'd seen ad nauseum. Among them all were the appendages, the dismembered pieces from what had to be mannequins, life-size plastic dolls, unplayable playthings.

Everything that met his eye was in some stage of disintegration, even as more flotsam tumbled in from rapidly widening oval slits located at various heights along the chunky, undulatory walls. He only noticed the almond portals when they were in a *mouthing* motion.

Each object's dissolution process seemed to speed up as he neared it—an impetus for him to keep moving, even if this was just a dream. Inanimate objects met their fate quickly. And in a lucid dream such as this, the sensation of pain was real. He'd no desire to experience death.

But maybe he could learn something. His subconscious seemed to be pushing a message. Was his day job too much for him? The dematerializing objects he'd recognized were all detritus from the mall. When spotting each item, he involuntarily imagined the store or kiosk from which it had come. His life, his *imaginings*, his dreams—they were all centered on the shopping mall. Maybe he needed a new job. Maybe now was the time to aspire to something greater, something more fitting that he hadn't thought of before.

But it couldn't just have been a secret burning desire for a sudden career change that had brought on *this*, the most realistic nightmare he'd ever experienced. Something chemical must have mixed with his hidden inchoate wishes to give them such vibrancy, such apparent solidity. Someone must have put something in one of his beers last night, a time-lapse capsule of some sort, a pill designed to knock him out and have its way with his subconscious, stirring up a nightmare . . . an experience he couldn't escape until he had the appropriate epiphany, or until the experience reached its necessary—and inevitably painful—conclusion.

Smithson, his fellow mall cop and drinking buddy, was a practical joker, but he wasn't malicious enough to put drugs this potent into anyone's drink. Who then? Who were his enemies? Who hated him so much? Or cared so much?

It was entirely possible that this was a tough-love prank by some hidden, long-forgotten angel from his past. Someone who saw he was on the wrong path and wanted to set him right, even undertaking extreme measures to do so.

He bounced various possibilities as he sloshed about the treacherous terrain, ignoring his lower leg pain, dodging obstacles, and reflexively cataloging the sights. Perhaps as he came closer to realizing his raison d'être, an exit from the dream would present itself and an easy path would blaze itself before him. Or perhaps he'd see and surmise enough to earn the discovery of a comfortable cubbyhole where he might tuck himself, avoiding harm, evading death, while forcing "sleep"—his actual reawakening into sober reality whereupon his reason for living would strike him like lightning.

As he carried on, however, an easy exit seemed less possible; a warm cubbyhole, a fetid joke. The raining barrage of gnawed pieces and chunks from his deadly dull life continued. But with each passing moment, the sights, while remaining familiar, took more effort to place.

He trudged among heaps of automobiles—an extravagant garden of makes and models—perhaps emblematic of what he'd glimpsed in the mall's parking lot during his lunchtime constitutionals. But what to make of the semi-trucks? Trailers and all . . . Or the garbage trucks? Dump trucks. A front loader. An excavator. A crane.

He saw all these only in pieces, enough of their metallic carcasses remaining for him to guess the whole. Yet, when meeting his eyes, they were still fragments, in varied states of decomposition. Construction sites weren't part of his day-to-day. Symbolic, surely; representational of his need to dispose of the old and build anew.

The helicopter, though, was a surprise, and difficult to interpret. Less so the coffins—some seemingly nailed shut while many others burst open to reveal lacerated bodies, expired flesh divorced from spirit. He felt some kinship. In this dreamscape, he wasn't much more than an undead man walking, plodding, framed irregularly, incongruently, by sheets of brick, tangles of metal, and conglomerates of glass shards.

Ever alert to his surroundings—his eyes snatching and ingesting—his imagination couldn't help but take these snippets of scenes and develop them into what they might have been, and what they could be. Banks, real estate offices, a post office, a bookstore, and other establishments that lined the main street of his hometown. His unforgotten hometown. Was his dream now sending him memories to help clarify possible futures?

What-ifs and how-abouts formed in his mind, materializing as if by a process of reverse-dissolution. His thoughts weren't only in his head but laid out explicitly around him—

a dreamscaped mind scraped and turned inside out. As fractured objects around him dissolved, his potential futures—once formed—remained fractured, less than whole, *damaged*.

He cursed his lack of fate—loudly, vociferously—even as he was met with a sudden onrush of polychromatic fog, engulfing him in a colorful murk as if to giving visual representation to his profane rant.

A small fraction of his consciousness noted the fog was suffuse with pea-size globules that felt and sounded like *bang-snaps* when touching his skin. They seemed drawn to the flecks. The snapping connections were more slightly irritating than outright painful. The true pain came in the form of regrets, the ones that stuck like burrs in the furrows of his brain. The image of such was vivid enough so that when the burrs burst—sending their shrapnel to other sections of his brain to sink deeper—he intermixed shrieks and anguished cries into his tirade.

His exclamations seemed to excite the fog, enough so that its colorful droplets jittered and spun in manners sufficient to briefly form multidimensional images—a wide variety of objects that stirred deeper memories. Henri wiped at his watery eyes, swallowed less and less saliva down an itchy throat, and futilely licked his stinging lips as he noted the phantasmal objects from a youth he mostly wanted to forget. Trudging on, he damped and spaced out his foulest language as he increasingly focused on wrong turns made in childhood, where those turns had led.

*Coming here* . . . Coming to this town and setting himself up in mall security was a mistake. That much was now abundantly clear. The malls were dying. A symbol of capitalism . . . a piece of America . . . a gathering spot for denizens of the Heartland to perform important rituals . . . *dying*. Like him, in this town.

His plodding feet now met softer terrain. Less wet, steadily more comforting as the colored vapor before him dissipated in confetti wisps, giving view to an expansive field of ridged clay abundant with tufts of flowers and broad patches of weeds.

He halted, inhaling deeply as he let his eyes graze. The air was different here, fresher. The expanse before him was reminiscent of Mingrell's Park. Located a few blocks from the mall, he'd frequented it often. To exercise. To contemplate. To pick up women.

To be put down by women. More regrets . . .

In waking life, the park was greener and featured a picnic area, children's playsets, an outdoor gym for adults, as well as plenty of smooth rolling space for strolling and sitting, kite flying and fountain wishing. A beautiful whole containing separate realms for fun, placidity, and adventure. But here, what structures there had been—lampposts, benches, jungle gyms, and fountains—were all out of place. Broken, crumpled, overgrown with a luminescent, greenish-orange moss.

In the air, hovering at various distances, were half a dozen spheres the size of exercise balls. To Henri, they looked like the free-floating eyes of houseflies.

Much higher above, the latticed dark-blue firmament resembled a misplaced fence—or a gate—one broad enough to block out yet give generous hints of the ash gray and embers farther beyond it.

Henri gave more attention to what was under his feet as he proceeded unsteadily into the ridged and furrowed expanse: reddish-brown clay and wild grasses. Weeds. Clover. Dandelions. Ground ivy. Forget-me-nots.

His skin seemed to approach the pale blue of the latter's flowers. The fog had shorn him of his shirt, leaving his tattered shorts as his only covering. Feeling neither particularly warm nor cool, he didn't mind. Seemed appropriate for a park. Comfortable. He missed his sandals, though. The soft patches of clay gave soothing respite between the flowers that tickled his soles and the blades that scratched his calves.

Henri kept up a good pace but didn't—couldn't—overdo it. The wide field provided abundance only to the sure-footed for wild running. It also provided plenty of space for playing games that penalized patience. Weeds choked, after all. The too-slow-moving. The look-at-mes. The procrastinators. The I-don't-knows. Henri kept it moving, heading in the direction of the area he knew best. An area where he might shift the shape of things to come.

The farther he went, the more the wildflowers danced, jittering like compass needles teased by children's magnets, all while his nostrils entertained the grassy and floral aromas redolent of early summers spent in careless play.

As he neared the adult gym area, however, gazing at its tangled, mossed-over equipment, he picked up hints of putrefaction, putting him in the mind of noxious weeds—those that were threats to health and property, overrunning one of his favorite childhood play areas, necessitating prolonged closures.

Closing in on the grotesque, he couldn't help but think of invasive weeds—those that overran ecosystems. *Entire* systems. Systems like America, which lived or died by its Heartland.

A few paces within its oddly comfortable radius, he halted, regarding the exercise equipment, mourning the time he'd wasted in waking life. He pondered the exercises he could've done, should've done. Other things he could have done. Other measures he could have taken.

As vaguely familiar aromas overcame him, scents at once fruity and medicinal, he spat curses at his usual routines—those patterns so ingrained, he'd never given them much thought.

There were substances he could have taken, chemicals he could have ingested into his system. Substances that could've enhanced his acuity. Chemicals that could have strengthened his muscles, made his bones and their configurations irrelevant.

*That's* what this dream was telling him.

He could've taken substances to numb the pain, to get him through the trials. He could've taken dosages—just enough—to impress his superiors, verbally, psychologically, and physically, all en route to surpassing them. He could've reconstituted himself, altering the processes within him to make himself into an überagent for Heartland Security.

He looked back toward the distant veil of mists—the polychromatic barrier between this area and the realm of dissolution.

The dissolution of objects, he surmised, were the dream's relation of life's end. The dissolving of the body after death. The everyday familiarity of the objects represented pieces of his soul. The soul and the body—there's no unity if one passes from this world without fulfilling a dream. Once the breath of life leaves the body—primary goal incomplete—the body disintegrates, the breath evaporates. The human run ends in oblivion.

The mind's relationship with the body is tenuous unless strengthened. Dreams and the imagination work to only give hints of the ideal . . . the ideal body. A regimen of the correct chemicals and doses of the proper ideas could make the ideal a solidified fact. A superior fact.

Distantly, a clamor arose to his left.

Narrowing his sight in that direction, he saw figures on the horizon. Scattered. Some immobile; others swaying; a few lurched within a constrained space, as if stamping out complex patterns on a game board. More than a few staggered off in multiple directions, lazily determined to find themselves away into some other space, some other game.

Henri figured his subconscious had called forth others to occupy this park—to recreate, and to aid in his own re-creation. His thoughts flitted, touching briefly on the folks he'd often seen in the park, before alighting on more famil-iars—his neighbors—those left behind in his waking life.

Lazily gazing at the dispersing mass of figures, he again considered the conspiracy theories batted about by his friends. He considered the strangeness of the war games and imagined himself—his enhanced self, his ideal self—in a similar scenario. One where he hadn't been drugged. A scenario that didn't involve play. No *games*. He imagined the town had been attacked.

Whether by accident or malicious intent, his town—his fellow citizens—had been the victims of a weapon of mass destruction. One possibly biological in nature. Or so he contemplated.

He'd read about such things. In the darker corners of the internet, a wide variety of cutting-edge weaponry was discussed; their uses, analyzed. The most effective weapons for governments to use against other governments. The most effective weapons for citizens to use against oppressors. The ideal methods of protection and assault for citizens against their rabidly irrational fellows. The perfect cocktails for a government to lob at citizens who refused to abide by the rule of law.

Henri had read about them all, in detail. In sufficient detail to consider that something, some combination of horrible things, had been passing through the town—perhaps on its way to Nevada, where it might be deployed against that apocalyptic polygamist cult he'd read about. In the middle of transport, something had leaked, exploded, conflagrated.

A few of the lurchers neared, proximate enough for Henri to size them up. Humanoid, yes, but greenish-gray, and glistening, as if misted with dew.

Henri stayed his ground, keeping close to the gym equipment, trying to deduce the meaning of their appearances, these drab staggering figures, arrayed from head to toe in what seemed to be brown bits of pine cone and interwoven strands of dulled aluminum and pine needles, most of which lay flat while some jutted outward like bristles. The approaching figures emitted faint vapors from their ears and mouths, and from their underarms and crotches.

A peaty aroma met Henri's nostrils as six of them converged. He likened their odd appearance to fatigues—uniforms for those out in the field, laboring. Soldiering.

An experimental bomb mixed with a biological agent—he imagined that *this* was the result. And he imagined himself spared . . . only to be tested now.

He took a step toward the approaching menaces, glancing at each of their faces, horribly mangled visages that managed to flash clear expressions of hate. He assumed a fighting stance, keeping his eyes more on their slick torsos and limbs as they moved within a few paces of him.

This was his Agency training. This was his do-over.

Succeeding at this would shove him out of the dream, back into reality.

He smiled at his realization—just as one of the man-creatures on his right lunged at him. A defensive spin and an outward thrust elbow were enough to send the attacker stumbling to the ground, though not without eliciting a wince and a curse from Henri. The man-creature's bristles were even sharper than they'd appeared.

As Henri recoiled in momentary shock, two man-creatures lunged for him. He sidestepped and clasped his hands together; another step and he swung the cross-fingered combination at the closest one's head, catching it in the face.

The other creature scraped Henri's leg. Henri hollered as he twisted to jerk it away, backpedaling two paces before launching a swift kick, landing a firm blow in his attacker's midsection.

With celerity, he maneuvered to put several paces between himself and the six while tossing glances toward the others who were slowing approaching. The fallen regrouped.

Henri's eyes darted, blinked rapidly, as he tried to control his breath, wondering why his dream-self wasn't in better shape than his actual self. Perhaps it would only be so with the right amount of concentration.

The peaty aroma grew stronger, pumping an occasional cough from his body as a dozen of the man-creatures formed an imperfect semicircle around him. They seemed to size him up, were perhaps formulating a plan, making Henri wonder if he could tap into their thoughts. As figments of his dream, why not?

The why and the how, he soon discovered, were two vastly different questions, with difficult answers. And whatever they were thinking, as they inched forward, it seemed that they'd concluded to keep up the attack.

Henri set his teeth. Swallowed. It'd be foolish to plunge himself in among them. And naked defense was no way to play. He'd have to make use of his environment.

Keeping proximate to the exercise equipment, he made several darting movements and intimidating motions toward each, trying—and succeeding—in drawing them to him.

Almost in unison, they rushed forward. Henri deftly backpedaled and maneuvered himself onto his chosen ground and worked his ploy, testing his body.

Dodging, dipping, and twisting to punch, kick, and sweep—he used the equipment to his advantage, as blockers and obstacles for the enemy. He tried to avoid bristles, did his best to avoid the pine-cone plating, and had to take care to avoid the falling and stumbling bodies.

Bodies that seemed to regather themselves much more quickly after each fall. Bodies that seemed to strengthen after each blow. Bodies that seemed to learn how to anticipate after one too many frustrations.

Henri's own frustration caught up with him, winding him as much as his exertions. Overconfidence and some plain carelessness tripped him up, but he recovered—the first few times.

They outfought him. Outfoxed him. He tried to take refuge by expending a burst of energy to clamber up a ladder and perch himself atop the monkey bars. Fending off any who tried to jump or climb after him, he gasped for air —air that increasingly seemed to carry the smell of frying meat—*beef*—overcooking.

He wished he had a gun. He wished he had something other than this mere body. A body of limited abilities.

Limited tactics, despite what he'd tried to will, tried to instill.

The smells of burning fat, sizzling meat grew stronger as he defended his perch—until a thought struck him.

He'd been going about this wrong. Now was a time for a *testing* of the ideal.

As the scents of cooked meat were joined by the putrid scents of overripe fruits and rotting vegetables, he inhaled deeply, letting it all in. Let the chemicals permeate.

When the attackers amassed into two groupings below him, he picked one at whim and dove in for a last dance.

Close-quartered sticking, dodging, and moving rapidly transitioned to tussling, a pile-on.

Overcome with bodies, new fragrances, and newer instincts, Henri began using his teeth and jaws more than his hands and feet. He bit; he hollered; he gnawed, growled. His inner man-beast attempted a philosophical feast in turn, chewing on regrets to give the body even more energy.

The wilder he got, the more the flecks that had been scattered about his skin and clothes seemed to expand in size. They tightened and loosened, each time growing bigger and seeming to go down a level, through the remaining clothing, through the layers of skin. So it seemed. Henri was too erratic, too ferocious, to pause and take note.

He got his moment of calm when he found himself on his hands and knees, heaving, smack in the middle of a shallow puddle of sewage-green glop. The oleaginous liquid dripping from his lips contributed reddish-brown swirls to the pool.

His opponents had let off and were scattering, off into other parts of the park, disappearing into the fog steadily encroaching from all sides.

Henri raised his chin but not his body as he watched his

opponents flee. He'd achieved some kind of victory—exactly what kind he was at a loss to say.

He'd tasted flesh—a rubbery yet tangy meat with metallic hints. He wasn't going to try to interpret. There was no perfect sense to be made of any of this. That would come in time.

He attempted to heave himself up to his feet but fell to sitting on his rear, trying to catch his breath while wondering if he'd ever gotten such a workout in a dream before, even in his anxious dreams during his Heartland Security training days.

He gave up wondering and started to give standing another try when something clamped the back of his neck and pulled him up to his feet.

Before he could register his surprise, the assistant had let go of his nape, circled in front of him, and encircled its other clamp around Henri's throat.

Henri could breathe, but only just so. His eyes functioned well enough for him to see the new creature—the fresh opponent—as it pulled Henri closer, setting them eye to eye. Familiar eyes.

There was no mistaking it. *Toby*.

Henri's thoughts warbled. His recent battle fell under a new perspective.

He'd been fighting those he'd once disparaged as the "green guys." Their supervisor had now arrived on scene to set things straight.

As Henri gazed into creature-Toby's unblinking eyes, the latter's mouth contorted, issuing gurgling sounds interspersed with words.

"*. . . unchanged . . . you . . .*"

Henri couldn't make sense of it and didn't care to as he kicked and chopped and scratched at the creature, his sight alternating between the black and white . . . pepper and salt . . . all-too-common seasonings of the flesh . . . this kind, *his* kind . . .

It had been *his* kind, those who kept a black-and-white worldview—in or out; fit or not—they had kept him from succeeding with the HSA. Henri would show him. He'd pass this test.

He struggled free, feeling skin from his neck rip away as he did. His holler of pain gave him a mad energy, pushing him to throw his entire weight toward the creature-Toby.

They both fell to the ground, rolled in sand, which gave way, plunging them into a loose-flowing amber liquid replete with miniscule bubbles, trillions of them, alternately working to buoy them and hurry them along some current as they struggled.

Henri's sight blurred to an orange-smeared black, but he didn't give up the fight, *couldn't* give up as he still felt his opponent in his arms and felt clumps—bristly and bothersome—sliding against him.

Deep in this ether, the volatile mix of Henri and his personified überenemy, stirred the liquid into a churn as the patches on Henri's body *bang-snapped*, lighting up, setting him aflame, igniting the engulfing concoction, engulfing him and his opponent in an inferno, cooking them both.

Henri released a prolonged and primal scream through the effusion of orange. His voice gave out as the orange faded to pitch-black.

He slowly regained sensation, gradually realizing he lay facedown on mossy soil. He had a body and limbs, but he felt something had fundamentally changed. He'd strength enough—just enough—to push up to his knees. He was warm, smoldering, but gathering strength.

Bursts of electricity tickled his joints, instilling a sense of giddiness as his limbs twitched. They crackled sporadically at first, but quickly settled into a pattern, working him. With each electric charge, he'd the notion of giving himself away to himself. He was redoubling, increasing in power as his inner charge guided him to rise to his feet.

He stood in a cleared space amid a dense collection of shamrock-green stalks—by his perception: ten-foot-tall grass blades. He stood naked, his skin's hue a collection of beige and bluish smears, his skin's surface pocked with pinpricks, pulsating red.

Standing, he recognized his back was straighter than it had been in some time. His chest, broader. His heart pumped the blood of a New American in the making. He was certain he'd the *stuff* that could easily be remade into the type of being necessary to secure the Heartland. He had reached the status of ideal dream-self.

It was now time for him to wake up, reenter the world.

Before him, through the stalks, a light shone—a distant honey-amber glow that steadily grew brighter, wider.

Something was approaching. Something bright. Something that—he just felt—was *beautiful*.

Quickly it progressed. Through the spaces between the stalks, he thought he could make out the figure of a woman, one clothed in the raiment of a star. An angel of the morning . . . bright as the sun when it slipped past the horizon.

But he was determined not to avert his eyes. He wouldn't cower. He wouldn't run. He'd stand erect, face forward, like the New American he was destined to be. With wide open eyes, he'd accept his prize. He'd embrace his glory. And with pride—maybe even with a broad grin— he'd awake to his new life.

The figure emerged from the stalks in all her blazing

glory. It was impossible for him to get a clear view through the golden radiance that surrounded, but he could make out her voluptuous curves, the wiggle in her step as she neared, the throbbing tomato-red gash right about where her lips should have been—and the conical crown that rested above her head.

As he set eyes on the crown, it exploded, releasing a rapidly dispersing cloud of buzzing black beads, each of them quickly finding their way toward him, toward the pulsing red dots speckling his body, as if they were targets, marks for the beads' plunging stingers.

He had no scream, no utterance of any kind as he writhed and spun, jerking and twisting, into the pliant stalks as he tried to beat the attackers away, fight them off. But they were more formidable than the opponents his own size.

As they injected him with fluids that ran their own patterns—convulsing him, contorting him—he had flashes of being assaulted by the entire human species, buzzing with chatter: malicious rumors, conspiracy theories, hateful gossip, backbiting . . .

Just under his skin, oblong beads ran frantic as his temperature rose. Immediate cysts established themselves as his skin warmed, burned, then boiled, bursting the cysts, finally coercing an unearthly scream from Henri that joined in well with the choir of hellish insects.

Their song eased into evanescence as Henri's body—drained of moisture, sapped of spirit—crumbled to dust, each particle left to the further machinations of the winged stingers.

TWO

The pasture's wildflowers were among the few signs of vibrant life in Remy LeStrand's general vicinity, but what fragrance they may've emitted to attract pollinators was no match for the distant creature's fetid offerings. A foul omelet of rotting eggs, putrefying vegetables, and decaying meat.

The air seemed to vibrate, as if even it couldn't passively withstand the noxious expression. Yet, Lieutenant Colonel LeStrand had no choice but to take a hit for his team.

With a long, studied breath, he raised his binoculars once more, temporarily trapping the malodorous air in his lungs to give the appearance to any soldier who might glance his way that, in face of the danger, he kept his shoulders straight and his chest puffed, a posture indicating a firm resolve to end the colossal beast, or to die trying.

At twenty-nine, he'd led a good life. Heroic thus far. But he was nearly certain he might not grow into his next decade.

For its part, the creature had finally stopped growing, had paused its forward movement. From a couple of miles away, with his naked eye, Remy could see plenty of the creature that in a relatively short amount of time seemed to have reached the size of an aircraft carrier.

It was hard to tell exactly. His perspective was off. With the binoculars, he could at least see some of the valiant efforts being made to prevent it from expanding even more. No one needed a creature the size of the Mall of America.

Exhaling, he lowered his binoculars and looked to either side of him, scanning the landscape of mixed grasses and spontaneous blooms. The winged insects and those closer to the ground were likely unbothered by the otherworldly invasion, but there was no sign of any furry creatures grazing, crawling, or even scampering. The tremors had warned, sent most of them scattering long ago. The near and far fences—broken or not—were of no consequence. And those four-leggeds that couldn't move quickly enough—the livestock that were more valuable to others than to themselves— were well into the process of being relocated.

Remy stood in the shadow of the heavy-duty trailer that performed as the mobile command unit—stable and fortified, yet able to move relatively nimbly when necessary. Nearby were a couple of the more flexible tactical command vehicles. The all-terrain sprinters were in the distance but not beyond his naked sight. Those quick vehicles had been able to outpace the creature when it was on the move and relay intel back to all interested parties, crucial information on the creature's probable path and what areas might need rapid evacuation. Air support had taken over that monitoring duty and—thankfully—the creature had no offensive against anything in the air. At least, not any that Remy had yet seen.

Regardless, air support's presence had caused the creature to come to a halt. Or maybe it was just resting. Whichever, the on-ground vehicles had pulled back and somewhat regrouped.

Surrounded by few military vehicles and a smattering of personnel, Remy cursed the recession then—more specifically and profanely—the paltry funds that President Sagan and her congress felt were sufficient to fund America's armed forces.

He was the highest-ranking officer on the ground, a commander of the so-called "spectral forces"—military men and women recruited from different branches and agencies, assigned to deal almost exclusively with domestic, supernatural threats. There were women and men who outranked him, one or two of whom he was presently reporting to, but they were all remote, out of sight. In the face of imminent danger, he was "the man." The man duty bound to respond to the call and go charging into the snarling face of danger. The lucky man.

During the predawn hours of the morning, the nearest Heartland Security office had picked up faint signs of a HotSpot in Oklahoma. They soon determined that an extra-dimensional creature was wriggling its way onto Earth—or so Remy had been told by one whose job it was to detect such occurrences. The office contacted Washington; then, while waiting for the communication to wind its way through the bureaucracy, they did what they could to locate the general area of the arrival point.

Special operations forces were dispatched for surveillance. Anticipating some sort of trouble but not knowing exactly what kind, they rallied local soldiers and law enforcement, prepping them as best they could until the spectral forces could be mobilized.

Confusion reigned. Matters weren't helped by the gradual and sudden shifts in the environment. As with all such beyond-the-depths creatures, strange occurrences near its point of arrival far preceded its actual appearance.

The creature had apparently entered this dimension in the vicinity of a condominium complex. According to the first responders' reports, it materialized amid a patch of multihued mist like a four-dimensional puzzle, shifting wildly in shapes, patterns, and colors, until finally finding some coherence in this world as a lugworm the size of a suburban two-story house, writhing out from its invisible sands, its feelers trying to find some stability as its viscid body inevitably got stuck on everything—brick, metal, glass, wood. What it couldn't (or wouldn't) shake, it absorbed, causing it to grow, inevitably resulting in more objects getting stuck to it.

Uprooted trees, vehicles, structures of various sizes—the absorption process was similar for all. Drained of color, the stuck objects became increasingly translucent and seemingly gummy as they slowly sank into the creature's beige-pinkish flesh. After several similar incorporations, Remy had come to understand that this process involved a pus oozing from the creature, coating the object as the creature's darkening flesh embraced it. Once an object had sunk to a sufficient level, the area of absorption simply appeared as an irregular mound on the creature's writhing body, a crimson and indigo rash overpopulated with several smaller bumps that eventually flattened.

As the creature acquired mass, it inevitably changed shape; as it changed shape, the creature inevitably changed its position. From writhing, to slithering and sidewinding; from finding a path that suited it, to creeping about to find another, all the while continuing its acquisitions and mergers. The environment grew increasingly hostile.

A second wave of ground forces had been deployed,

backed by close air support. Other forces worked in tandem to evacuate all residences and businesses, with special operatives using a variety of means to enforce a workable media blackout. "Strategic corporals" headed these efforts and, based on their frequent check-ins with Remy, seemed to be doing just fine. Obscuration was the Heartland Security Agency's specialty, after all, and it was much more easily accomplished in the less populated areas of Middle America.

Small blessing the creature hadn't appeared near a major city. As it was, the casualties left in its wake numbered only in the thousands. Four digits. But he'd little faith the casualties wouldn't increase exponentially before this was all over. To Remy it seemed the supply of blessings, big and small, was dwindling these days.

Since being promoted and moving to Texas a year ago, he'd received periodic briefings, each more depressing than the last. Dimensional breaches like this one used to be rare. Over the past few years, they averaged about one per month somewhere in the world. Over the past few weeks, however, they'd increased to about one every other day, most of them happening within or too near the nation's borders. Each nation had its own dark methods of dealing with such matters. The United States was no exception. In fact, the people tasked with protecting the slowly disintegrating states felt obligated to go further than what others were doing—or were rumored to be doing—further and much deeper than the president, her congress, or her court could ever see or comprehend.

The governor had yet to declare a state of emergency. Remy's job was to ensure the situation didn't reach the point where such a declaration was warranted.

While others sat and paced inside the heavy-duty

vehicle behind him, studying screens, delivering information through his headset, he preferred to be out in the same air as the creature, faintly thinking (wistfully hoping) the breeze might waft his way some hints of the creature's weaknesses, along with some ideas as to what items or methods at his disposal might exploit them. Thus far, he was clueless. Hapless.

But not hopeless. Not yet.

Presently, the creature looked like a hodgepodge of slimy hardbacks, a conglomerate of gargantuan snails. Gazing upon it now, Remy regarded the creature as a dragon from another realm, an ugly tourist taking a rest from its rude binge, perhaps reflecting on whether it could actually live here and live well.

It had tried to adapt, had tried to sustain itself, had tried to become one. But now—supposing it had the capacity to do so—it was rethinking its options. The living hadn't been easy so far. Perhaps it was figuring how to act less out of instinct and more out of reason, out of cunning. It was probably taking a better assessment of its new environment and determining how to conquer.

Luminescent coils nestled in the creature's swirling carapaces. The bewilderment of patterns strained Remy's eyes, throbbed his brain, but he focused on them enough for their slow-spiraling and gentle pulse of greenish light to give him the impression of gills. He figured those fleshy springs were attempting to process an atmosphere that couldn't possibly be congenial.

Its skin was also dotted with pustules that emitted short yet frantic propulsions of frost and flames. Many but not all had gone dormant since the creature came to rest.

A rainbow's array of extruding tubes—clusters of them, sparse and dispersed about the creature's hide—had manifested during its resting period. They put Remy in the mind of sea anemone, leading him to believe that maybe the creature had decided to set roots right where it was. The foul stench emitting as a faintly visible vapor from small, irregular hexagonal pores was perhaps further confirmation—or maybe just a sign of the creature relieving itself.

And here Remy stood, taking it all in. The duty-bound man. The struck-lucky man . . .

*Can a man change his nature?*

He wondered. Often. If one were born with an urge to protect, to defend, to perform service in the preservation of an idea, pushing toward the establishment of the ideal, would change be as simple as changing one's mind? Could such change happen naturally? Drastically? A swift left turn toward serving an idea of protecting oneself . . .

From the time he'd seen his father mown down by an inebriated driver, something stirred within him—as if his soul had been struck by lightning, seeding and quickening it so that a new sense would rapidly blossom. A sense of divine fairness. Justice. His father—a god-fearing teetotaler who'd supported a family of four with his work as an electrical engineer—had been served something else. He was no saint in Remy's recollection, nor even in Remy's at-the-time nine-year-old mind. But who had warranted such a violent fate? And what kind of human being would intentionally get intoxicated on a Tuesday afternoon—summertime be damned—and take to the roadways, only to careen off into a parking lot, barreling on through the plate glass window of a hardware store?

It had all happened in a flash. Three were killed. Two (including the driver) were carried away, sustaining minor injuries. One—at least one—was miraculously unscathed. Remy had been so near to the accident and yet, mentally, so far. It was a freakish experience, one in which only he and his father existed; then, in a snap, only one of them did. Physically, Remy was able to walk away. Psychologically . . .

He recognized fallibility, was familiar with instability. Even if he didn't have the vocabulary for such words at the time, he understood their meaning. So he couldn't sustain hate. Couldn't harbor blame—at least not for any extended period.

The man who'd crashed through the hardware store window had been a recent widower. He'd been lost without his beloved, lost without the one who'd reminded him and guided him when it was time to take his medications. Separated from both his primary sources of stability, he rapidly slid down the path of becoming lost to himself. He couldn't find his pills, couldn't recall the name of the prescriber, couldn't find any notation on where the prescription had been filled. But he was in pain—so *much* pain—physical and psychological. He had to numb himself, just long enough to find his way to a pharmacy or a hospital, whichever he encountered first. The hardware store had gotten in the way.

Remy got the full story later in life. By then he was in his early teens, and on a timer. Set to exact some sort of change in the human species. Wide-ranging, if possible. Limited, if necessary. But change had to come. It was necessary for humanity's survival and progression—the *ideal* of what the species should be.

Were some members of the species unnecessary? Were some just too debilitating, too destructive, inching the entire lot of them toward some sort of mass extinction? Were those who let these harmful types go unchecked unconsciously assenting to a consensual suicide? He'd spent twenty years in study and observation trying to find the answer, all while training himself to fall into a role where he might help exact the necessary change. The necessary justice.

And that had been part of the problem. He never figured out exactly how such an internal revolution might be exacted, let alone the specifics of what the changes should entail. So his only suitable role was in the field, where he still searched, still pondered and studied, while fighting and protecting.

Men needed to protect themselves from their inclinations—particularly the inclination to preemptively eradicate the potentially destructive and otherwise troublesome among the species. But had he been following the right path? The path that had led him *here?*

The beast had been assaulted with conventional and nonconventional weapons. Some chemical; some not approved for use on American soil—at least not officially. Many of the true threats to American society didn't officially exist, after all. Regardless, the assault had done little. What the spectral forces had done up until now had been ineffective. If there was a time to lay on the truly heavy firepower, it was now or never.

Apparently, he wasn't alone in his assessment.

A *zing* struck his nostrils a moment before the sharp, sweet flavor flowed onto his taste buds. He recognized the fresh aroma of an oncoming rainstorm as his gaze traveled upward.

At least half a mile above the creature, hovering orbs manifested from nowhere, each of them appearing like gargantuan Easter eggs, wildly decorated with colorful yet shifting streaks and crazily playful squiggles. He counted five before they descended, hurtling toward the ground as they rapidly shed their coverings in colorful streamers of light.

Each color-stripping egg was a translucent pod by the time it landed upright in the dirt, in close proximity to the creature. Each one harbored a passenger.

As Remy adjusted his binoculars for a better look, the giant egg-shaped bubbles popped, permitting their now-freed inhabitants to scramble into action.

It seemed the communications of dire straits had snaked further along—winding and sidewinding—to the upper echelons while simultaneously tunneling deeper underground, reaching the men and/or women responsible for facilitating the *darkest* of America's black ops. And now that the black proficients had finally arrived, it was like a sudden storm.

He'd never met them—but he'd been briefed. He knew them by sight, and by action.

There was the woman who screamed musical notes—literal, visible red-and-blue notes—that cut like paper-thin razors and burned like fire or ice when slicing.

There was the guy who ran, leaped, flipped, and danced at a dizzying speed, all the while flinging arm-length lightning bolts that each hit their target as precisely as the mythical Robin Hood's arrows.

Much farther back from the rest was the little girl who walked pensively, reading from her sacred diary—a tome of words written in blood on patchwork pages of animal, plant, and human skins—which caused her targets to combust, explode into mists of disparate foreign colors, or freeze and shrink into compact crystalline figurines.

There was the man who seemed to take hold of wind, light, and shadows, sculpting them into an army of black-and-white intangibles able to outwit almost any opponent, great or small in number.

Likely there were others assaulting the creature from

another front, or otherwise beyond Remy's range of vision, but all of them—seen and unseen—were part of the black ops group known in need-to-know circles as the Dark Artzmen. A pet project of some big shot HSA official in Washington.

Their reputed feats and accomplishments were impressive.

Their showing today, less so.

It soon became clear they weren't doing much more than inspiring awe and anxiousness in Remy and likely any others who witnessed their futile efforts.

The bolts of lightning (or whatever the bolts really were) did little-to-no damage to the creature's patchwork skin, let alone the shell; the slimy coating seemed to deflect all attempts.

The singing woman's notes managed to neuter some of the sea anemone; but Remy's enhanced vision confirmed his fear of them slowly growing back.

The little girl accomplished a slightly bigger victory, extinguishing both the flames and frost that had taken so many lives and devastated so many homes, buildings, and trees; but she apparently couldn't shrink the creature, nor explode any significant parts of it.

The sculptor, it seemed, was reduced to using his abilities solely to prevent damage to his fellow Artists.

They and their compatriots seemed lost, wandering far from their reputation. But they kept their courage.

The Artzmen had been audacious to get so close to the creature, and they'd remained fearless as they fought. Remy could detect notes of frustration among some, particularly when the dancer fell on his face, tripping on a slime trail. But they were something, and they were on the verge of becoming something else entirely once the sky began to darken.

The rainstorm aromas returned, stronger and intermixed with floral scents as silence overtook the landscape. There was a complete absence of sound as silvery green clouds manifested from nothing high above the creature, as if trailing from unseen cigars smoked by an equally invisible conference of giants.

Remy had never before witnessed the coming, but he knew of the signs.

*The archangel.*

The Artzmen stopped in their tracks, tilted their chins upward.

The clouds seemed to conceal miniature suns . . . brilliant orbs that took a violent turn as the clouds acquired a purplish hue.

The temperature fluctuated between what felt like a summer's day in Arizona and a winter's night in Quebec. His skin itched, as if strings were wriggling over various parts of his body. But he'd the soldier's discipline to remain still as the newly formed clouds amassed, betraying the influence of a rotating column of wind. A low whistling slid into the silence like a long blade, growing into a pervading scream as the mass of clouds extended a corkscrewing funnel from its purplish base.

As the twister touched down on the top of the creature, it seemed to penetrate, an occasion celebrated at other various points around the beast by explosions of air and eruptions of its skin.

From these breaches of the creature's hide, mad crowds of four-winged bipedal creatures spilled out, and the Artzmen scrambled to engage them, recognizing them as the threats they were.

The Artists regrouped to work as a team, arranging themselves like the bright points on the constellation of a heavenly hero brought down to Earth.

The girl made crystalline warriors out of the sculptor's wind, light, and shadow creations. In turn, these creations acted as receptacles for the singer's notes and the dancer's bolts, converting them into even more powerful projectiles that they methodically launched into the riotous crowds of winged creatures.

The thunderous claps continued as the air became increasingly populated with unsettled soot, glittering detritus, tossed this way and that. Before Remy completely lost his sight—or something even more dear—he retreated into the mobile command unit behind him.

It was time to get his own forces to regroup and lend the Artzmen whatever assistance they could among the hordes of creatures their own size. They'd leave the slaying of the bigger beast to the angel from beyond space and time.

# THREE

Neal felt like he should be dumber than he actually was. A low-level Heartland Security agent, undone and remade, to brush shoulders with supernal beings tasked with reordering Creation after the death of God . . . His had been quite a promotion—one for which he hadn't exactly applied.

And yet here he stood among the similarly initiated in an otherworldly war room, raptly attuned to absorb a briefing on why God's death might happen sooner than any had anticipated.

Standing to Neal's right was a man who could use wind and other elements to create brigades of ghosts wielding laser weapons. To Neal's left was a woman who spoke in song, each of her words manifesting as a flying insect of light, each and every one of them ready to sting or bite, injecting dangerous levels of radiation into a target.

They and five others possessing unique abilities with some connection to light and sound had congregated in a wide room of seven sides. Black ovals and other portals of varying shapes, each radiant with dull colors, lined the transparent crystalline walls. The walls themselves permitted a view of the haze beyond: depthless, bluish green, and overpopulated with black phantomlike streaks.

Neal and his compatriots were more than comfortable were they stood, despite the fact their very souls were on display for a being whose very aura was fear's musk.

This being—a sentient amalgam more properly designated as a Calvarian—was using its entire body to project animated holograms, each of them emitting unsteady hums. The projections' untidy rhythms neatly served to impart knowledge that supplemented the harsh words conveyed by the Calvarian's booming voice.

Standing more than a dozen feet tall, the Calvarian had a roided-out male bodybuilder's torso and arms. Its brownish-gray midsection was crowned with the long neck, crackling mane, and belittling mazzard of a fierce unicorn. Its teeth were a composite of glass and metal. Its equine eyes glowed a vivid, soul-chilling blue; Neal and the seven other figures arrayed before it did their best to neither flinch nor shudder when falling within its line of sight. Sturdy horselike legs and hooves complemented the Calvarian's head and neck—yet it possessed hands reminiscent of a bird's feet, the talons of an osprey. A wavering turquoise-blue radiance, evoking fluttering robes of sheer silk, swaddled much of the Calvarian's midsection.

The horrifically beautiful being had no proper name, only an honorific designation: *the Equinox.*

Beyond its appearance, Neal had little understanding of the full range of its abilities. He understood only that the Equinox served as "consultant" to the eight in the room and several others beyond it who, collectively and colloquially, were known as the Dark Artzmen—a black ops group comprised of supernaturally gifted soldiers who neglected armor, uniforms, camouflage, or any mundane clothing. In their reworked bodies, none of it was a necessity.

Like the other Artzmen, a portion of Neal's soul had been reworked and repurposed as his new skin, giving him the appearance of a living chess board. The skin was a comfortable fit, so long as he didn't gaze at himself.

As if by reflex at the very thought, Neal glanced at his hand. One finger black with ice-white nail, another finger white with coal-black nail . . . The white-and-black checkered pattern continued across his hand, up his arm, and all over his body. When careful, he avoided the sight of anything that might reflect his entire self.

Endowed with the ability to generate limited-range force fields and to cast expertly woven nets of light that could work a variety of wonders, Neal considered whether these or any of his other abilities would be enough against the enemy at hand.

The Equinox had designated their monstrous target an "Arigrian." Its origin was the depths of XynKroma, the deepest dimension—a roiling realm of polluted light that served as the end point of every living creature's mind; the oceanic terminus for the rivers of psychogenic energies fed by all sentient beings' streams of thought (noticed and not). Every living being's hopes, fears, desires, hates, wishes, and everything else along the psychological spectrum mixed, fought, and blended with one another in XynKroma, resulting in the birth of other beings—archetypes and symbols at conception yet rapidly unfolding and developing into all manners of beasts, creatures most at home in altogether indomitable environments.

Neal knew the portals to XynKroma were numerous and treacherous. And traffic could flow both ways, as the Arigrian had demonstrated.

The Equinox had gathered Neal and his fellow Artzmen together in a meeting room encapsulated within an interstitial bubble that bobbed between various levels of Reality. The insulated, irregular sphere had been created by the conscious effort of another being, one adept at manipulating light, space, and time within favored environments.

The construction and design of the structure of which the war room was just a part lay beyond Neal's comprehension—but he envisioned it as a multidimensional globule; an air pocket trapped within stained glass. Stained glass—he figured—was as good a description as any for certain levels of Reality. Those on Reality's surface—human beings, primarily—were always looking out upon a painted world, even when peering deeper out into what they called "outer space."

If only the glass could be made clear so that humankind could see all of Reality's potential wonders and horrors, perhaps human beings might begin to comprehend the truths hitherto hidden from their conscious selves and work to prepare themselves for the inevitable moment when the glass shattered altogether . . .

Then again, maybe it was just as well that humankind remained blind a little longer. How would those on Reality's surface handle it if the manifestations of their deepest thoughts took notice and looked back at them? As the Arigrian had shown, not too well. Matters would only get worse.

The Arigrian sustained itself, at least in part, on two related yet very particular strains of humankind's thoughts: *Doubt* and *Regret*. Manifested now on Earth due to the boundaries between the dimensions becoming so porous, the creature was perhaps unintentionally engaged in a bacchanalia. But it was no celebratory occasion for anyone else involved.

Neal and the other Artzmen had learned that the barriers between the levels of Reality were becoming increasingly more passable. Unless the process could be reversed, a devastating flood would occur—an eruption of the deepest, darkest thoughts from the mind—resulting in the realm of *Heaven&Hell* (and all its creatures, ranging from the barely comprehensible to the impossible) overrunning all, ending the process of God's Creation.

Neal knew as well as anyone: the stakes were not low.

Presently beyond the crystalline walls, out in the bluish green that he referred to as the "ether," a violet ball of lightning zagged and zigged, weaving among the phantomlike streaks as if taunting them into a dangerous game.

When the ball suddenly frizzled out of sight, the Equinox dismissed the others with a rumbling word and, with a gesture of his talon, signaled for Neal to remain. The others noiselessly proceeded toward the walls' black ovals, which swallowed them whole. The disappeared Artzmen would be transported to somewhere within proximity of the Arigrian where they'd, hopefully, put their talents to some use.

Neal followed the Equinox to a free-standing, twenty-foot-tall, mauve rectangle. Passing through, they proceeded down a short corridor that corkscrewed them into another passageway, longer and narrower, its boundaries a sizzling gray foam as cloudlike in appearance as it was firm to the touch.

Sparsely populated with amethyst beads, the foam—Neal quickly learned—was not to be ogled. A peek into any of the purple gems opened an internal eye, giving him sudden and multifaceted bird's-eye views of every Artzman currently in action anywhere on Earth. After two such dizzying forays, he avoided even a glimpse at the foam; the amethyst pebbles were decorations too valuable to be seen, let alone pondered. He narrowed instead on the Equinox's dark bluish mane, which sizzled, as if each thread of hair were an incipient lightning bolt ready to strike out and lay low some enemy.

He didn't dare when the Equinox's blazing cold eyes were on him, but Neal couldn't help but take this opportunity to focus on the horn. It was like iridescent nacreous shell, honed into an extended spear tip. It shifted between colors but favored greens and pinks, an odd complement to the predominant brownish gray of the rest of its form. Though, to Neal, "odd complements" might've served as a good summation of the Artzmen membership and affiliates —consultants included.

Although to any outside observer they might seem to coincide, the relatively recent formation of the Dark Artzmen was not due to the various and very recent manifestations of beings from XynKroma. Rather, the black Artists had been the long hidden brainchild of a Heartland Security agent—highly ranked, yet exponentially influential above his station—one who'd simply wanted to establish a force beyond the known armed forces, a strike force that would be more effective against terrorist threats of supernatural means.

This agent and his collaborators were particularly fearful of The Infinite Definite, a loose collection of terrorist cells whose members had a special relationship with XynKroma. These perversely gifted horror-mongers carried terror to new levels: outsider art fornicating with outré violence, working a variety of blood-sex-light-magick spells for the singular purpose of merging all levels of Reality into chaos.

By the time the Artzmen had been recruited and coalesced into an effective black ops unit, The Infinite Definite had made significant progress in achieving their goal; hence the rapidly multiplying invasions of creatures from beyond. Despite all he knew, Neal hadn't been too worried about the multiple breaches. Though they often seemed outnumbered, the Artzmen had a few magickal aces in the hole. The Equinox was just one.

As it led Neal down a zigzagging path through iridescent veils, the silky turquoise-blue radiance that fluttered about the Equinox's form seemed to shift and stiffen, giving the momentary appearance of hundreds of ephemeral wings jutting from its backside.

At a glance, Neal considered that such miniscule wings fluttering every which way would not aid the creature in flight—but that conclusion was born of the residual rationality of his wholly human self. The Equinox *could* fly, and the tiny wings might very well be of use.

Then again, what he was seeing could've been merely for show, a reaction to something in the passageway that went undetected by Neal. Or it could've just been Neal's sight playing tricks on him. His body had been reworked— but it was still a body, still had senses. And though many of his old human senses had been enhanced, he retained a few of their old weaknesses as well.

Still, Neal understood that the Equinox was itself a hybrid—an enchanted byproduct—the remnant of a human child's soul that had gotten sucked into XynKroma while attempting to flee some human-conceived terror: a child killer, or a child rapist. Maybe both.

While in XynKroma, this forgotten child's soul had

tried to stay hidden. But with the soul's gelatinous properties—semitransparent and tenacious—it could not avoid learning, *experiencing* the ways of the dimension. By the soul's very state and nature, it was inevitable that fragments of the weird environment would pass through and that some pieces would stick. As a survival tactic, the soul could not resist incorporating bits and pieces from the phantasmagoric environment, physically and otherwise, making them a comfortable part of itself. Yet, at some point, the steady if prickly osmosis was interrupted. A creature native to XynKroma discovered the errant soul, was bothered by its presence, and thus challenged it. The child's soul held its own in the ensuing violent struggle until another creature intervened and acted as adjudicator. A bargain was struck. The Equinox was born.

Neal's personal history was less mysterious, far less interesting—to himself at least. He cared more for the story still to be written.

He halted behind the Equinox, who'd stopped before a wall of multihued mist too thick for Neal to see beyond even with his enhanced abilities. When he made the attempt, his vision scattered, sending him a multitude of incomprehensible images before refocusing on his own face.

He let off trying, focusing again on the Equinox, who said nothing, only gestured. Responding with a respectful nod, Neal walked past the creature then suddenly halted.

Before he could determine whether a deep-down fear held him back or some outside force, he felt three pinches about the crown of his head. It was the claws of the Equinox, who'd grasped his pate from behind. The acute pain quickly gave way to a pleasurable vibration, a sensation that remained for a moment after the Equinox released him from its grip.

Neal did not say anything. He didn't even turn to see the Equinox continue on its way. The Equinox had left him with a parting gift, one he'd need for the mission to come.

Neal stepped forward, into the mist. He withstood a tickling wash before emerging into a rotunda with a generous circumference.

Here, as in the corridor Neal had just left, amethyst beads seeded the foamy floor. The ceiling was similarly afflicted—but that barrier was beyond Neal's ken. The walls would neither cohere, nor stay put. They were free-floating, slightly concaved, silvery white hexagonal plates the size of patio screen doors that constantly slid, shifted, and shuffled around one another as they projected holographic images: detailed, multidimensional, yet miniaturized happenings of scenes all over the planet Earth.

. . . at least from Neal's perspective.

The four plates nearest him projected scenes of chaos: mob scenes in what appeared to be India; riots in what was possibly some east Asian nation; street fighting in some European country, based on the background buildings' architecture; and masses of people in some rural area confronting what could only be described as a trio of creatures approximating scorpions, each of them the size of automobile sedans.

This entire semicylindrical space was a monitoring station for the chief Artzman, the one flying high above who —at initial glance—appeared as a fierce tussle of violet-hued and phoenix-feathered birds; feathered fiends as madly in love with themselves as they were jealous of each other. *Saint Valentinus*, an archangel.

The archangel had ostensibly been tasked with leading the Artzmen, but Neal knew his true goal was drawing the Final Map, figuring the geography of peace and harmony among all surviving forms of life in the aftermath of the Apocalypse—the Death of God. The steady weakening of the boundaries was increasing evidence that such a cataclysm was approaching. Not only was time of the essence, but the essence of time was dissipating, fraying the veils between realities, introducing incongruities, puzzlements, bizzarities, and outright horrors into many corners of the everyday world. The tipping point of humankind's derangement—God's Last Breath—could come at any moment.

The Artzmen were among the initiated. Protected and would-be protectors of The End's survivors. As a former Heartland Security agent, Neal had been made privy to the secrets of the angels, the knowledge kept from those who knew of and would wield the power of the Artzmen. Still, he gazed in wonderment at Valentinus—his one-time foe turned *savior*—engaged presently in a complex multidimensional dance-fight to save souls.

Here, beyond human consciousness's consensual space-time, the archangel monitored a multitude of incidents on Earth, deciding when and where to intervene. Sliding, slicing, and twirling about like a winged figure skater on airs thick with unseen and unbound ice crystals, Valentinus flicked wisps of the amethyst light from his body.

These hurled flames were essentially outlines of the archangel that grew into simulacrums stretching out to reach, embrace, and dance with the plates' projected holographic scenarios—an inholy spirit tussling with cold-fiery images, becoming enwrapped and engulfed in silent sparkles and luminescent waves—until the holographic scenario fully embraced the angel's simulacrum, incorporating a replica of Valentinus every bit as knowledgeable and powerful as the original into its scene. From the perspective of those who existed in the actual scenario,

Valentinus—a version of him—would suddenly manifest, striking through a violet and electric-blue tear in thin air. Each version existed as one of many, all of them connected and ready to be reabsorbed into the prime source once they'd performed their limited duties.

Each such embrace of simulacrum and scenario shuddered the cool air around Neal, shivering his body. Yet he neither changed his position nor said a word, just did his best to maintain a respectful stance while he watched, awestruck.

Valentinus sent forth at least a dozen representations to various points on Earth before his primary self deigned to notice Neal and descended, his archangel wings thrust backward like an alighting eagle.

Stopping to hover a dozen or so feet above and in front of Neal, the eight-foot-tall archangel's fiery wings jutted from his back like proud flags of love-peace-and-war that burned without being consumed. Flickers jotted out and away from the shifting wings, sifting colors from violet to indigo to greenish yellow, as the remaining body appeared primarily as a composite of wolf and man—the latter's features assigned to the archangel's torso and arms.

Valentinus narrowed his wolfish eyes on Neal's.

Neal's insides reflexively rippled. Yet, he maintained his posture, as any self-respecting and duty-bound soldier would.

"I had hoped we would not need so many on one enemy." Muted rumbles of thunder accompanied the archangel's words. "Not this soon."

Neal's insides rippled again, this time urging him to chuckle—a reaction he rapidly suppressed. "*Soon*" had been the tickler. His concept of time and its passage had changed greatly since he'd become acquainted with the realms of angels and their affiliates.

"The more seasoned Artists," Valentinus thundered, "have only the skills to contain the creature. Not end it."

Neal frowned but quickly corrected his expression as he thought, *What does he expect me to do?*

Seeming to read his mind, Valentinus said, "You need to attack the *heart* of the creature."

Neal's head slowly shook. "But that's *your* thing . . . isn't it?"

"In this instance, it shall be *our* thing." Valentinus's eyes momentarily blazed red-violet. "The Arigrian's heart is not like the heart of Earth creatures, yet it serves the same purpose. To keep its vitals flowing. I will get you inside." The archangel drifted closer to him. "I know this will only be your third mission as one of us—but I have confidence in the full spectrum of your abilities. Untested though they may be."

Which, Neal figured, is why the archangel deigned to come address him directly rather than sending a version of himself to do it. Still, he'd mentioned the obvious. Neal had acquired many abilities during his transition from mere human. Many of his new talents were sourced from a particularly strong flavor of psychokinesis, which undoubtedly was the reason Valentinus felt he was ideal for going inside the belly of the beast. Though Neal certainly knew how to use his abilities, he'd used only a select few in the field, and he'd yet to use them against a serious threat. The Arigrian was a serious threat many times over.

Valentinus's eyes flared a deeper shade of violet. "Is there a problem?"

Neal queased at the archangel's tone. He hadn't bothered to suppress any expression of consternation. His face undoubtedly told the angel more than enough already. But Neal couldn't lie. "You're implying that I'll be inside this beast alone . . . Shouldn't I have a partner?"

"You will have *guidance*. If you believe there is anything missing, it is simply faith."

Neal's chin trembled slightly. He was grateful, at least, his new skin tone prevented the angel from seeing a flush creep across his cheeks.

"The Equinox briefed you on the creature's provenance and implanted within you a tool that will assist your mission. As we journey, I will impart what I've learned of the Arigrian's anatomy. Come."

Valentinus lunged toward Neal. Before the latter could flinch, the archangel had gripped his shoulders and lifted him off the ground.

They rose, facing each other—the angel staring down, Neal's head tilted back—their eyes locked. The dance began.

Neal felt as if he was suddenly engulfed by a massive rush of autumn leaves battered by fierce gusts of rain, the storm's winds and waters a mélange of unalluring voices working out an incantation.

Valentinus's abilities of space-time displacement not only allowed aspects of the archangel to simultaneously exist—fully and completely—in multiple places within a limited time range; it also allowed him to cut up specially seasoned slices of the grand hyperdimension of XynKroma and temporarily remove them from their space-time continuum, setting the slices as traps under his control. Traps for his prey. Or for his recruits. The space-time traps served as topsy-turvy realms devoted to training. Or torture. Neal had been among the elite few that had been subjected to both.

When initiated into the corps, he'd been glued to such

a trap—beaten and taught, fought and lessoned, turned inside out—for a period that seemed to last two or three years. But according to the way time ran on Earth, he'd only sojourned in the realm for less than two days. Time and space had lost then gained entirely new meanings to him—but in the here and now, he was in sync with the situation. He was uniquely aware of the threat the creature posed. He knew exactly from where the creature had slithered. Neal had trained only in an outer level of XynKroma, but the information Valentinus was transmitting during their dance took him to a new level of adequacy.

As he and Valentinus twirled, Neal became lost in the fusillade of crisp images, engulfed in the nipping wisps of spaces and times from across the Earth, each time-space experienced just long enough for him to sense they were fractions of tumultuous scenes—women, children, and men caught up in turmoil. When Neal realized he was being exposed to the scenes of the Arigrian's rampage and its victims, the chill on his soul burrowed even deeper.

Valentinus imparted his knowledge of the creature, not through words, but a code—a tangible static Neal felt at the core of his being, a static that frizzed in opposition to his outer self. As Neal gained in knowledge, he felt and saw himself dissolving, disintegrating into smaller and smaller black or white globules, each of them steadily acquiring the taint of the colorful time-space wisps. Though separate, the painted globs remained in proximity to one another, making Neal feel relatively whole.

Gradually his vision pulled away from himself to focus on a grayish smog, which soon cleared to reveal what seemed to be a field of snail antennae—hundreds of eye-tipped stalks swaying and stretching.

*The Arigrian*—from above. Just a small section of the creature's hide.

Neal's form remained a loose cluster of undulating blobs as his entire separate-but-related-self experienced the general sensation of flowing down a spiraling staircase.

He was coming in fast on one spot: a relatively bare patch amid the tentacles. The closer he got, the more he realized the stalks were crowned not with eyes but with what appeared to be human heads—though he couldn't determine with certainty as the stalks were swiftly mowed down to clear his landing spot.

A shower of droplets joined his descent, each drop as sharp as a glass shard yet sparkling like a polished gemstone. Rushing past him, each drop burst and dissolved upon impact, sending up whiffs of vapor. The gem storm acted as an acid, eating away at the affected calico surface as Neal neared, washing the red and white into pink, diluting the black into gray.

Valentinus was not within Neal's range of vision, but the archangel's presence was apparent to him.

Streaks of light shot past Neal from behind, striking the pinkish gray patch, tickling it with brilliant bursts that momentarily brought lilacs, orchids, and wisteria to Neal's mind as the patch became increasingly translucent.

Neal understood that Valentinus was tenderizing the hide while simultaneously paralyzing the patch, channeling electromagnetic static to prevent the creature from making any attempt to assimilate Neal as he passed through what was now a thin membrane.

The pieces of himself gathered into two strings of black-and-white beads—two upright chains that coiled around one another as the beads melted and reconstituted, melted and reconstituted, continuing the cycle as they steadily resolved themselves into a solitary humanoid figure.

Neal felt as a vivified puppet twirling on strings rapidly fraying and snapping. Becoming himself again, he continued to turn slowly in an imperfect circle, taking in his new environment.

His visual talents were impaired here inside the beast. He'd have to do without telescopic, x-ray, and other abilities he'd normally trigger by a mere squint and some concentration. Thus far, he could see well enough around him, even though the atmosphere was tinged with a rose-pink haze.

He was in a space that he gauged to be the size of a baseball field. The ground was thick with short, soft filaments. Though the bristles were black, Neal likened it to Astroturf.

Hovering about at varying distances from each other and the ground were globes possessing the girth of yoga balls and the appearance of fly-eyes. Neal counted five. Every so often, several dozen spikes jutted out from seemingly random ommatidia of the compound eyes only to swiftly retract back inside.

Overhead lay an uneven swatch of glistening mesh, like a crosshatch of metal wire and freshly spun spider's silk, evidence of the creature's body rapidly repairing the hole made by Neal's entrance.

*Spin and observe . . .* He was now on Reality's surface—but deep inside a creature that had emerged from the depths of Reality, a dimension unknown by and imperceptible to the vast majority of those who resided on Reality's surface. *Head, spin . . .*

He took tentative steps in one direction, altered his course toward another direction, then adjusted again, subtly guided by the *spinning intuit* with which the Equinox had gifted him—a map-and-compass sense that had lit up and begun to work now that he was inside the target.

The intuitive sense jerked and tugged. Acute impulsions drove him onward.

Neal didn't possess an exact map of the beast's anatomy. Such exactness was an impossibility due to the creature's accumulations and growth. But there were constants.

No matter how many modifications were made to the human body—how many limbs amputated, how many senses failed, how many screws or plates inserted—every human being required certain organs to keep them alive. The creature also had its necessary organs.

What Valentinus had referred to as a "heart" didn't pump blood. The creature needed no such fluid. Its "blood" was immaterial and transmitted via different channels, carried not by arteries and veins, but by the hovering fly-eye spheres. The periodic outthrusts and retractions of the prickly spikes were visual signifiers of the creature's pulse, the pumping and channeling of the ingredients that supplied energy, encouraged growth.

The compass aspect of Neal's new sense tapped into the creature's circulatory system and, with each pulse, conjured an increasingly detailed map of where Neal needed to go—the direction he needed to take, if not the dangers he'd face.

When drilling through, Valentinus had attempted to deposit Neal near one of the hearts, but the creature's internals had shifted by the time Neal had gathered himself. Still, he wasn't too far off.

With an increasing rhythm of impulsions, the sense guided him toward a wheezing fissure—a cleft amid a massive reddish-beige wall of bulging folds and deep grooves.

Neal widened the gap farther by thrusting a series of psychokinetic spears—successive force fields shaped and sharpened—whose tips unfolded like golf umbrellas, each of them building on the other to inflate the circumference.

Passing through the gap, he stepped into a breezy cavern replete with bronze spider crickets the size of house pets.

His old sensibilities again.

The chirping hoppers weren't crickets. They were something that had been consumed and modified by the creature's body, perhaps to supplement its digestive system, cleansing the system of impurities. Impurities small enough for them to handle.

Or perhaps they were just signifiers of an immune system building itself as the creature's body became accustomed to a new realm.

So long as they paid him little mind—leaping out of his path as he made his way through the mass—he gave them the same, lending more of his attention to the fly-eyes.

He spotted six, but the atmosphere was murkier here, tainted with a burnt-orange hue. Neal breathed in a different fashion than humans—he could survive where others would suffocate—but the humid air gripped him, slowing his pace as he proceeded on footing less comfortable than the black bristles had been.

The ground here was gritty—like a thin layer of sand lying on asphalt—and irregularly trembling, as if powerful motors lay just underneath its surface. He managed well enough, even as he heard faint sizzles and crackles, the familiar sounds of faulty light fixtures.

The noises grew steadily louder as he trod a gradually upward sloping course littered with fractured stones.

His map-and-compass was leading him toward an enormous hovering mass in the distance—a gigantic pinwheel unraveling into a loose ball of rubber bands becoming further undone. *The heart*. More accurately, it was a combination of pieces of the creature's brain and heart—and just one of many. Each of the heart-brain structures were connected with one another, relying on one another to keep the creature healthy. Additional structures would form and grow as the creature continued to acquire size and mass, becoming more accustomed to its environment.

What seemed to him a floating spaghetti toss of cords twisting and writhing around one another was soon obscured by billowing peach smoke, like a dense collection of sunset-tinged clouds that loomed as a grand tower before shifting, putting Neal in the mind of nebulae.

The Carina. The Omega. *Beautiful*. Wondrous.

The sight also put him in the mind of skies stained by the setting sun, natural works of art he'd enjoyed the most during his prepubescent years—summer evenings spent down in Alabama with his cousins, sitting in backyards and chomping on watermelon wedges, flicking the seeds at them (and them at him), chasing fireflies, chasing each other, and shouting out first-thought plans for the night.

They'd been good times. Fun trips.

Until the summer his dad baited and switched him.

Like every summer, they'd driven down to spend a week. Once the week was up, his father had asked if Neal would like to spend an extra week with his cousins. His father would drive back to Illinois and drive back down a week later to retrieve him.

Neal readily agreed. It was the summer after sixth grade. The lack of parental supervision would provide some much-desired time to blossom a bit before entering the all-important first year of middle school. He'd have time and space to consider whether he needed to adopt a new persona, season his personality a bit to appear more mature to his peers. Astronomy had been his chief interest then—but he'd need to start thinking about getting a girlfriend for the inevitable school dances, not to mention other activities. A week with his cousins would be sufficient for him to have fun while contemplating how and if he needed to mold and shape himself into a new young man, one ready and willing to make a new name for himself.

But one week stretched into two weeks. Three. Then four. As his father repeatedly—cruelly—promised during their Wednesday night phone calls that he would come soon. But "soon" was nebulous.

His relationship with his cousins and their friends was much clearer when it came to time. The times of their lives. The fast times spent during a too hot summer. In dank basements. Clammy bedrooms. His young cousins were older than him. More experienced with adult life (and lies) than him.

They'd always joked about the regional differences between their upbringings. Their differing slang. Their differing ambitions. Now that they had him under greater influence, the jokes blackened. There was talk about him catching up. Fitting in. He'd have to obey their tutelage if he wanted to hang with them. Enjoy the summer with them. All the free time . . .

As the weeks dragged, it became harder to resist. He ran out of excuses for saying "no." He ran out of excuses for saying "wait." He ran out of breath.

If only he'd been stronger. If only he'd been raised better. If only his parents had taken more time with him.

The one week had multiplied into eight before his father finally returned—all smiles—to bring him home.

Neal's summer had been taken from him. So much had been taken . . .

Had his father known what would happen? Had his father known his brothers and sisters—Neal's uncles and aunts—would give their children free reign? Neal had never even attempted to discuss it with him. But he still remembered how hard he'd glared at the grinning goon of a man. Such a fierce gaze today would flash-freeze his father, holding the man steady—holding him accountable—while his innards combusted.

Neal shivered at the thought.

He shivered again at the realization.

The creature had gotten to him.

*Doubt. Regrets.*

He'd been walking up the gravelly slope as if afflicted with snow blindness. His vision had blurred, gritting up his sight and memories with jagged scenes of youth. Just discolored snippets; some of the most painful. Now, his eyes watered. His head throbbed. His mournful trudge . . .

He had to pause.

Recognition was only the first step in combating the creature's assault. The second was to push back, push out of himself. The Equinox had been a more than capable instructor.

His skin flickered as he imagined tartan patterns, focused on them as radiation filtered through his soul-skin, mixed with *Intention*, and was expelled, appearing as multiple colors crosshatching around his body, gradually settling on translucence. The result: a snug and unencumbering armor, psychokinetically forged and strengthened by his manipulations of electromagnetic radiation.

It would now be far more difficult, Neal figured, for the beast to play with his mind.

He proceeded on, trembling with each step. He reasoned it was just his body getting used to the armor when sudden gusts—crisscrossing and powerful—took hold and lifted him, spinning him around, tossing him off-balance. Before he could determine which way was up, let alone perform any defensive maneuvers, he was thrown atop a patch of sand.

He got to his feet as rapidly as he could, blinking as he looked all around, readying himself for a more tangible enemy than a localized tornado. Nothing approached him—but his environment was new.

The surrounding terrain was a bleached-sand desert behaving much like a windswept lake. Ripples of grains coursing in one direction, then another.

There were no fly-eyes in sight. Instead, the stale air was sparsely populated with spiky lumps the size of human hearts, rust-hued and moving in erratic patterns, leaving glimmering trails of vapor in their wake.

Curlicues of vapor arose from Neal's body as well. His armor was gone; the concentration needed to maintain it was lost to the gusts. Now, a thin layer of liquid coated him, a lubricant for the loose hairs gliding about his skin. His body was normally hairless. He figured the oil had the same function as saliva in humans—predigestion. But what of the threads?

He moved a few steps in one direction, then another, trying to stir the map-and-compass, get it working properly. But the threads—*it had to be the threads, those mockeries of loose clothing*—were throwing off his newest sense, making him dizzy.

He continued his dance nonetheless—a few steps in one direction, then another, and then another. The loose threads likely had the purpose of keeping him lost, spun farther and farther away from his goal until the beast was ready to fully absorb him—a process that could begin at any moment. The sand beneath Neal's feet was soft enough to give way with each step and quick enough to bury his foot and harden before he could lift it to take another step. He quickened his pace, but the trapping sand tripped him up more than once.

The vapor rising from his body was a sign of it reflexively trying to cleanse the oil and threads from its surface—but the process wasn't working quick enough. Neal decided to give it a boost.

He concentrated on the threads, connected with them telepathically. They were mindless; the only thing he could read was their purpose and weaknesses. His skin flickered again as he drew in radiation, filtered it, and expelled it as a tight-as-skin head-to-toe force field containing just the right dosage of radiation that was anathema to the threads. They fizzled from sight.

*Stability.*

He felt more himself again. But despite the slithering strings being absent from his body, he was still lost, cut off from his map-and-compass.

He trotted in a circle, steadily spiraling out his path while taking care to evade the spiky lumps. Neal figured —*hoped*—when he hit upon a direction that was most correct for him, the beast would counterattack with a new and unique defense.

It wasn't long before the spiky lumps all but retreated from his presence and he found himself jogging near a patch of semitranslucent globs, hovering just above his head, bobbing to and fro. Each glob encapsulated what appeared to be a melting artifact from an office building—a desk chair;

a keyboard; a drawer from a file cabinet; a desktop fan; a wastebasket . . .

He slowed and shifted his course. The path he needed to travel was through these.

He wended his way through, wondering at the items and learning quickly that, after an object inside a glob melted fully, the glob itself rapidly shrunk and exploded. The bursts had a small range, but Neal ensured he kept the globs at a reasonable distance as he maneuvered through their congregation.

The creature's internal defense mechanisms were as varied as they were unpredictable—but they weren't random.

The creature could not only shift its shape but alter its entrails in response to threats. The Equinox had termed one of the creature's inner defense mechanisms as downcycling —repurposing specimens that it couldn't or wouldn't outright consume, utilizing them for other purposes that were beneficial to itself and detrimental to invaders. *Noted.*

As a hissing smog encompassed him, enshrouding everything around him, he prepared to protect against what he couldn't predict.

His skin reflexively adjusted, coating him with a defensive force field of moderate intensity, shielding him from any bursting globs as he moved cautiously forward.

On Reality's surface, he could easily see through the dark and solid objects; but his suppressed visual abilities here did him no favors as barely seen tendrils whipped at him from various directions, sparking and shocking upon contact. Owing to his force field, the blows were more irritating than painful—but they weren't attempting to burn him.

The tendrils were fighting to wrap themselves around his neck, his wrists and arms, his legs and ankles. As he pushed forward, Neal batted away most attempts. Even when they managed to entangle, he snapped and unwrapped them before they could do any serious harm. Affliction wasn't their purpose. Neal realized their intent was to distract and slow him as he stumbled about the smog—itself a soup of foul odors and hateful voices, condensed. A black noise working as a very visible acid.

He'd known what he was walking into—the end result of it, anyway. The trick now was to keep up his defenses and muddle through before the beast had its way. The beast seemed to be making more progress than him.

As random areas on his skin began to burn, he concentrated on tartan patterns, *focused* on encasement as the radiation filtered through him.

The beast pushed back, attempting to smother him in a dense, scalding broth.

An unending and uniform shriek sounded in Neal's ears, drilling at his attention.

His knees buckled, but he remained on his feet. He couldn't, *wouldn't* go down.

Neal raised his hands, holding them inches from his face. The black patches of the pattern sucked in his gaze, drew in the totality of his concentration as the white patches pulsed, growing ever brighter—radiating, healing, protecting.

His skin cooled, tingled pleasurably. He even tasted a hint of peppermint.

Brief periods of silence broke up the fire-detector shrill in his ears. The shriek eventually gave way to the dulcet tones of birds at dawn, sounds that segued to the chirping of nighttime crickets before a thunderous grumble silenced them all.

With another longer rumble the beast yielded. The smog dissipated as Neal closed his eyes to gather himself. Using any of his abilities was taxing. Some took more energy out of him than others.

When he opened his eyes, there was no trace of smog. The once-snapping tendrils now lay flat and unmoving like dead snakes among the upright grass and fallen dross of the new terrain.

He was in a forest—a longleaf pine grassland. Or an environment that remarkably resembled one. The generously spaced columns were as tall as longleaf pines, but they curved and twisted rather than reaching straight up. Clinging to them were miniscule creatures displaying the white-and-black horizontal stripes of red-cockaded woodpeckers. There were abundant clumps of grasses that looked very much like the bluestem grasses commonly found in western Alabama.

*Alabama . . .*

Was Neal manipulating the environment, or it him?

*Head, spin . . .*

His map-and-compass was back on track, so he moved as briskly as he could, jogging through the grassland, pondering the new environment.

He understood that much of what was experienced on Reality's surface by its residents was just that—the outermost surface of things. Obfuscators. Distractions. Vanities. Yet he vividly recalled his time among the benighted, back when he was fully human. He again felt like one of them.

What he saw around him—how much of it was real? How much could he manipulate, and what was beyond him?

Everything his old fully human self had experienced— seen, heard, tasted, smelled, considered—had been taken in by his mind only to be spun off, weaving a personal reality that made some sort of sense to him. Pieces of new experiences snatched and matched with older experiences to comfort him, or teach him, or even coerce him to react.

Humans may, at times, share a physical space—but they never share the same reality. Thus lovemaking, as most humans practiced it, was a lie.

Maneuvering around a "longleaf pine," he envisioned strolling through a real pine forest, a real forest of any kind; two would-be lovers on a nice romantic stroll, exchanging sweet nothings while inhaling the scents of wildflowers. Herbs. Wild mint. Evoking natural perfumes, a back-to-nature romance, one involving Mother Nature, the provocative aromas redolent of . . .

*Chemicals.*

The creature was redoubling its efforts to assimilate him before eradicating him. He thought of pushing back, but the creature might simply do the same as before, plunging him into a whirlwind assault of the senses, shoving him farther from his goal. His compass told him he was close, so he decided to gamble. He'd hold off from pushing back, from expending more energy than necessary, unless the going really got tough. In the meantime, he'd lean in, reminiscing about love, and its many facets.

*Love will save us all.*

Casting glances at the woodpeckers and a more distant fly-eye, he let his inner guide glide him around the treelike columns as he recalled the not-too-long-ago days (and nights) of frequenting dating websites, all the time spent seeking interesting matches. He used to indulge in elaborate fantasies about meeting and connecting with the right woman, finding the spark that would set off an inferno of joy and bliss for the pair—a happy, passionate, yet also painful process of adjusting so they'd fit together perfectly, living their remaining lives as one. A smoldering perfection that would result in them giving the greatest gift to themselves and the world: children.

When he joined the Heartland Security Agency, he'd believed wholeheartedly in the goal for which it had been founded: to help stem the tide of disintegrating families, which led to more and more wayward children, children who grew up only to get caught up in promiscuity, drugs, and violence. Despite the taunts of critics who claimed to be for social justice, Neal had found no irony in wanting to be a Peacemaker—an armed enforcer of the Agency's mission. Proof was all around that the world was going to pot; the unravelling of the social fabric was the ultimate cause, and strong, stable families would be the solution. Sometimes it took more than propaganda to fight the good fight, especially when there were so many armed gangs and other outfits peddling illicit substances and promoting disease-spreading dalliances. Creators of orphans, enablers of runaways, flesh traffickers—the list of dangerous enemies was lengthy, but not daunting.

What had frustrated Neal had been his lack of success in establishing a family of his own. Prior to his conversion by the archangel, Neal—despite his bona fides and his HSA credentials—had been the enemy of Order.

Disregarding his parents' advice to pursue his long abandoned scientific ambitions—and essentially cutting them out of his life—he took up the pursuit of defending the American ideal of a family: husband and wife, two to three children, and at least one dog all sharing space in a stand-alone home whose only hints of disarray would be the toys occasionally left scattered about the well-manicured lawn. Despite the dangerous missions, the ideal seemed a lot easier to defend than for him to actually create such a prized existence for himself.

Valentinus had his own plans for a family, a grander plan: facilitating the birth of the Child who'll bring an irreversible end to all the chaos. The birth would take place in an extradimensional temple-palace. And, in preparation of the universe-saving birth, the realm of the temple-palace would be populated with lost souls—souls that needed saving; souls that would be preserved for a peaceful life after the Apocalypse; souls that would bask in a Love they had never known.

Through his current (yet faint) link to the archangel, Neal sensed that Valentinus was nipping at the Arigrian from the outside, drilling, excising, and taking what he could from whatever humans were still alive within, plucking souls like an oxpecker picking ticks from a water buffalo. And the other Artzmen had rallied, as it seemed some smaller creatures had spilled out from the beast. Together with the military forces, the Artists were doing what they could to contain the hordes of once-human creatures that Valentinus could not save.

As Neal progressed, the treelike structures had grown straighter, thicker in circumference. The area also darkened as Neal's map-and-compass brought him to the base of one column in particular.

He puzzled before the grayish-brown cylinder, wondering if his spinning intuit was off-kilter. This structure—whatever it really was—was not one of the beast's hearts.

If he'd been outside the beast, he'd be able to easily x-ray the structure. Here, he could only step closer and place his hand against it. Something inside pulsed, as if calling to him. He placed his other hand against the cylinder. The signal was stronger. He began to push—only to feel scores of needles darting about on his skin.

Neal fell back with a holler, yelling less out of pain and more at the shocked realization that the creatures that looked like woodpeckers had somehow silently swarmed him.

He spun about, swatting at them, blocking and repelling them with bursts of limited force fields.

But they kept coming, most of them only momentarily stunned by Neal's defenses.

He didn't have the time or energy to waste on distractions.

Vacillating lights enveloped his skin as he attempted to armor himself while refocusing on the stout cylinder. He threw a combination of punches against the surface, cracking it. He then kicked at the same area, damaging it even more.

The peckers swarmed him.

Neal threw all of his weight against the column's damaged area, breaking through the surface and stumbling inside.

The peckers had left him. They gathered just outside the entrance he'd made, but none even attempted to dart in after him. Neal tuned out their fierce vocalizations—a loud and rapid succession of *sklit* sounds—while he examined the cylinder's inner lining: a tender azure flesh of some earthbound-yet-undiscovered fruit. He likened it to kiwifruit.

The signal was strong here. He lifted his chin, gazed upward. He had only one direction to go.

The bluish flesh was as soft as it appeared, more waxy than spongy. He could insert his fingers, attaining sure handholds, without having the flesh rip or give way. He climbed, tentatively at first, testing the flesh's malleability, before scaling at the speed of an athlete in his prime.

At the top, Neal was met with a mass of salmon-pink rubbery tubes. He extended a series of psychokinetic tools—force fields successively honed and reshaped—to widen gaps and find passageways as he eased his way through. The tubes were slimy to the touch, but more glutinous than slippery.

Curlicues of vapor rose from his body as he emerged onto terrain similar to what he'd walked before. The cavern's atmosphere was murky, tinged with auburn. Yet, through it, Neal was able to spot three fly-eyes. The acute impulsions were as painful as they were pleasurable.

He proceeded along the rocky floor as if swaddled in a heavy blanket, the thick broth of the air making each movement forward a labor.

A population of the bronze creatures that resembled spider crickets leaped about, seeming to fold and unfold in midair, slightly increasing in size with each hop. They cleared a path for him as before, but amassed behind, following him as he plodded along, up the gradual slope, toward the enormous sizzling cloud.

Determining them to be of little threat, Neal paid them little mind, and even less as he entered in among a loose gathering of hovering, semitransparent globules, reminiscent of bloated jellyfish, each containing an item one might find in a big city's gift shop. Branded coffee mugs. Furry clumps that may at one time have been posable stuffed animals. Linked shimmering stones signifying cheap jewelry.

The Arigrian was working perversions, mocking him. Like a cat with a mouse in its paws and jaws, teasing the hapless creature before devouring it. But Neal was no mouse.

The globules were easy to evade, but not ignore. Though Neal didn't know their precise purpose, he tried not to care as he picked up his pace. He would not be deterred. He was close, *so* close to his goal.

The levitating globules full of worthless trinkets, odds and ends, all with smeared logos, indistinguishable branding . . . They were just trifles. Ridiculous gifts. None of them would compare with the final Gift.

The gift of the Child's existence would be a gift—ultimately—of Love to the remnants of humankind.

Neal had never gotten the opportunity to make a gift of his own body, had never gotten the chance to fulfill the meaning of his human existence: to procreate. Ultimately, he'd been divorced from the human population—too soon, or too late?

To have such thoughts while traipsing through the innards of such a creature, thoughts that stirred (almost) beyond his control . . . This was no gift. But Neal pushed on, forward, to give glory to the Gift to come.

Neal had been taught that humans have the ability—via genitals, procreation—to *image* in their bodies an earthly version of supreme *Love*, to give the greatest idea *flesh*, to make it incarnate. The Arigrian's emergence onto Reality's surface was not making Love an incarnate reality. While it existed, it worked only in opposition. It was the archenemy. *The Adversary.*

As Neal drew closer to the variegated cloud concealing its heart, the atmosphere curdled, became turbulent with the heavy and competing scents of vomit and spoiled milk. Loud groans and their echoes filled the cavern, accompanied by shrieks of pleasure. Grating giggles.

The hovering globules receded from his route only to be replaced by levitating orbs, perfect spheres the size of his head, exotic in hue and design under their transparent skins, much like a child's marbles.

More mockery.

It began as a tourist trap. A trap for one who'd only toured the American Dream of a happy, healthy family, one who'd never gotten the chance to make it reality. A failed father who'd never gotten a good start . . . The beast had transitioned from tourist trap to child's warped playground.

Plays. Dioramas. Vicious exhibits. These were the beast's own unique antibodies—internal defenses manifested as grotesque landscapes.

The beast had by now figured multiple ways to defeat a regular never-say-die human trapped within it. But not an Artzman. Not Neal. Not this one-time man who'd been an affront to the Creator, to His universe . . .

Though the "*His*" was a failure as well. "*He*" failed to even exist. There was no "Father" deity, and what was considered the "universe" was just a grand misinterpretation by humans on Reality's surface. Creation had never had its proper definition. Not among humans anyway.

Valentinus had taught him that a verse was composing Creation. Creation had begun when the Creator created Itself by beginning a Verse that was still being sung-spoken-written. Creation didn't happen but was still happening, developing as the Creator is being consumed by Its own Art. When the Verse ceases, running its natural course, the Creator will have fulfilled Its purpose, ceasing to exist as Creation reaches its endpoint, the End of History— universal peace and happiness for all. That was the intent, anyway.

The Verse—the process of Creation—spawned creatures originally destined to inhabit this blissful state, creative yet imperfect creatures whose deranged thoughts and toxic emotions exceeded boundaries and seeped into the deepest dimension . . . It was these creatures —*humankind*—who were tainting the process of Creation. They would bring about the Apocalypse as their habits disrupted the Verse, prematurely ending the Creator and the process of Creation, resulting in chaos, with little hope for peace or happiness.

Hence, the Artzmen—the uplifted creatives. Those who, with elevated guidance, could help recover a damaged work (or world) and make it anew prior to the arrival of the Gift. The Apocalypse couldn't be stopped, but many could be saved.

Neal had learned all this from Saint Valentinus in a *blink.*

When Neal blinked now among the levitating orbs, he saw snap-glimpses of his past. Memories. Dreams. Desires. All twisted.

He had to focus on the Verse. The Child's birth. The Gift. He had to focus on what was ultimately important in order to push on, keep going.

Ascending the increasingly steep slope, approaching the towering column of persimmon vapor as it gave way in parts, Neal glimpsed pieces of the heart-brain structure.

What had earlier seemed like a tussle of giant, twisting cords now appeared as woven, multihued strands of colossal ropes vertically spiraling around one another, each sparsely decorated with incandescent ovoids as if the ropes were necklaces of oval-shaped gemstones twirling around one another inside a merchant's display case. The unobscured ovoids' radiance brightened the area.

This very well could have been a different heart from

what Neal had witnessed earlier. For his purposes, it didn't matter. They were all connected. One heart was as good as another. The only question was whether he was good enough . . .

In the ovoids' light, his thoughts were a scramble, a free-floating tangle of strings that weren't limited to his head but seemed to float around him, tightening into knots that seemed to lash at his body as he tried focusing on what he needed to do. He thought of solar flares interfering with electronic communications. He thought of the projected scenes of chaos he'd witnessed in the archangel's monitoring station . . . How would they shake out with the primary Valentinus preoccupied with the beast? How would Valentinus fare if Neal failed? What would become of the Artzmen?

How often had Neal failed before?

Had he been right to cut off his relationships with his parents?

What of his cousins? Shouldn't he have been trying to save their souls? Wouldn't that be the *true* art—the artist working to save the souls of those who'd committed the most grievous wrongs on the artist?

Doubts . . .

*Doubts.* That's all they were.

The beast was redoubling its consumptive efforts.

Neal fought through it, tried to—but paused, shuddering, before stumbling to the left and right. He stopped walking altogether to focus on maintaining his footing as the cavern trembled ever more violently.

A fissure opened in the ground before him. Neal stumbled backward as it widened, and a shimmer of dust fell from high above, as if from a massive yet unseen hourglass. Once the cavern settled, Neal found himself gazing at a swath of sand. A desert separating him from the heart.

The levitating marbles rushed forward and fell into the sand as the spider crickets that had been trailing him leaped forward into the same, changing their shapes as they spread out. Neal watched them, waiting for the hopping creatures to settle on a shape, settle on a position, or at least a pattern, before he proceeded.

He considered the pouring of the sand, wondered what it really was, what outside materials the creature had consumed in order to produce it. He considered the toxic emotions pouring into XynKroma . . . And this beast, this archenemy, born of toxicity . . .

The crickets hadn't settled—but he wasn't about to waste time.

Colorful crosshatching lights enveloped him as he concentrated. Armored, he stepped forward.

Despite the sand's appearance, and the manner in which the crickets danced on it, the consistency was more like quicksand to Neal. His plodding feet were submerged, but his body sank no farther.

His pace however had slowed. The ovoids' brilliance further colored his thoughts. And the crickets settled on their shape . . .

Children and teenagers, kids of various ages and sizes, playing in the sandbox—a box filled with the remains of their own would-be parents.

Some of those humans consumed and repurposed had their thoughts read, analyzed by the beast as they were being downcycled. The children they would have produced in some now nonexistent future had been conjured here—images of them—to frolic in the ashes of their intended-but-now-never mothers and fathers.

Such were Neal's thoughts as these menacing images of offspring encircled him.

He couldn't back down. He couldn't hold back. He was too close.

As they converged, he turned in a circle, his eyes meeting each of theirs multiple times as he tagged every one of them, taking their radiation signatures, marking them, tightening his links with each subsequent glance. The black patches of his soul-skin pulsated as he forged connections.

When the offspring quickened, rushing toward him, Neal unleashed a refined radiation, focusing on the constellation that his opponents had formed but that he was determined to name as he connected the points between them—strengthening, sharpening, and shifting the lines—carving the on-rushers with fierce lasers, cutting and burning until they'd been reduced to pieces as atomic as the ashes underfoot.

Neal fell to his knees, came close to prostrating himself, throwing a series of prayers of forgiveness . . .

But to whom? There was nothing to pray to. Yet, the memories of his humanity were vivid enough that his body heaved, as if ready to open the floodgates, letting the tears flow.

*If only I'd been stronger. If only I'd been raised better. If only my parents had taken more time . . .*

He couldn't weep. Physically couldn't—and psychologically *wouldn't* allow regrets to let the Arigrian finish its job on him.

They hadn't been real kids. Those from whom the images had sprung had been real—but Neal hadn't killed them. And there was nothing he could do for them. He could only try to prevent any more humans from being extinguished in the same manner.

He was weakened, but he rose, fixing his gaze up ahead.

He had a mission to complete. The heart was such a short distance away.

The Adversary had thrown its worst at him, and failed. A sure sign was the hardening sand, the firmer ground under his feet as he moved forward.

But the air rumbled.

Neal slowed, watching in awe as the true protectors of the heart emerged out of its enshrouding vapor.

Undoubtedly intent on blood sport, the horde of dark angels descended.

FOUR

Henri felt *One* now. Of a piece. At *peace.*

Here was his place . . . Here, among a series of pocked walls of immense heights yet limited widths, partitions that were staggered like halfway-open doors without frames, each one leading only to the next.

Each wall boasted hundreds of octagonal-shaped cavities, each one filled with a kaleidoscopic light holding a body in suspense. Henri's was among them.

The other suspended bodies appeared to his eyes as dancing shadows, all grooving to unique rhythms and beats. Every so often a shadow would crumple into a malformed orb and shoot from the cavity, only to have its high-velocity flight paused in midair. As it hovered, the amber orb would slowly unravel, spooling downward like a thin, unbroken strand of honey, regathering itself into a new shape down in the abyss.

From his vantage, Henri could not see the end shapes or the floor of the abyss—but the inner connection they shared allowed him to intuit what was happening down there, and why. They all had a role to play. An assignment in service of the highest purpose. An assignment to which they'd tacitly agreed when their screaming souls petitioned to be saved.

In the eyes of the other observers, Henri no doubt appeared as just another shadow dancing in a phantasmagoria—but he felt abuzz with memories, swift recollections of all the deeds that had led him to this place, flitting snippets of his life darting and sparking in his mind. All the others were experiencing something similar, an experience unique to them.

Henri's thoughts, now, were on the taunters—those who had taunted him at the mall, at school, throughout his life, attempting to belittle him. *Can taunters haunt from beyond the grave?* He'd never considered the question—but all of them, all of them who had yet to be saved, were more dead than alive, even if they still walked, still talked. They were living in a false reality, a shared dream of low aspirations, an unreality filled with hate, fear, and despair.

The New American Dream began *here*, inside this body he shared with others who were hyperawake, inside this body that had given them new life, inside this body that they each had a part in keeping alive. They were a part of the body of the New World, the New America, the New West—the dragon that would consume all, the beast that would have control and rule over all. Henri and others in his colony had important roles in ensuring that the body worked well, performed as it should, and flourished.

It was now his turn to be deployed from his nest— ejected to pause, hover, and drizzle down into the obscure abyss. Whether by an exertion of the remaining fraction of his own will or by the already established design of the *One*, his consistency was less like honey and more like tar as he oozed down through the tangles of what seemed to be a suspended briar patch. More than a few thorns and prickly vines latched on to his substance and were carried through till he reached the flat ice that served as the floor of the abyss.

As his substance gathered on the frozen ground, he shivered himself upward, into an ambulatory shape, incorporating the vines and thorns into his new form as he solidified into a bipedal being with two arms ending in talons. Two pairs of wings thrust from his upper back. A cold liquefied light coursed through him.

His final shudder was one of frisson as he took in his new surroundings: a misting wonderland of arched crystalline structures, golden puddles, and pale-green vegetation. A few dozen others—bristling with prickles, four sharp wings jutting from each of their backs—populated the landscape. Their large yellow eyes made a glancing acknowledgment of one another, then, as a loose group, they lurched forward, some of them flexing their limbs as they moved, taking a short hop with every other step; others leaped to test their wings, gliding not too far above the ground.

They each moved differently but toward the same destination. They'd been instilled with one primary task: enter the old world in the name of the *One*—the newfangled serpent. Out in the old world, they were to shadow-buzz towns and cities, descending on populations dense and sparse, remaking everyone *fit* to share the Dream.

In their colorful cells, Henri and the others had been well prepared for their mission of slashing up humans and animals in such surgical ways that they would naturally combine with one another, becoming new creatures willing and able to process brick, metals, and other inorganics, turning them into materials the beast could more easily assimilate as it went about securing the land.

The external projectors of toxins that had been

converting trees, flowers, and other vegetation into something suitable for absorption were being disabled. The One was also experiencing other external assaults. Henri and his compatriots had a secondary task, a short-term mission: annihilating the outside disruptors.

Before they could act, they had notification of yet another disturbance, *inside*.

The shared internal urgings that had been gently guiding them toward the portals that would launch them out into the world stopped, cut short by what felt like an electric shriek pulsing through them. Trembling silently in pain, Henri watched the others around him do the same. The agonizing shriek stopped almost as quickly as it began, and a new surge pulsed through them.

Their wings flexed, lifting and propelling each of them off into various directions. The One was under dire threat. Henri and his compatriots were being roused to eliminate it, posthaste.

Henri's swift flight took him through a series of milieus until he passed through a rust-hued cloud and arrived over a landscape of fine rock fragments possessing shades of red, green, and brown.

His attention was jerked from the pleasant landscape to the wretched invader.

The dire threat they were to eradicate was a lone being, a figure with the body of an adult human male sans genitalia. Nude, muscular, and bearing a skin tone unlike any other: a chessboard arrangement of shining white and light-swallowing black. A games player. A creature from another dimension out to wreak havoc on the dragon of the New World.

As the others dove toward the invader, Henri held back, observing. With some concentrated focus, he could see the threat's skin was awash in a crisscross pattern of innumerable colors—too many, at least, for Henri to attempt to count or classify. He did, however, narrow his focus enough to perceive the alternating bands—oscillating waves—that produced the otherwise imperceptible pattern.

Owing to his links with the others in his colony, Henri knew his compatriots saw only the black and white and thus underestimated the being beneath the skin. The invader was outnumbered and somewhat sluggish compared to Henri's compatriots. But he was better coordinated. He seemed to have a plan of defense superior to their plan of attack.

As Henri studied the invader, his gaze alternated between the black and white . . . the soul-sucking pepper and the soul-crushed salt crystals . . . the all-too-common seasonings of the moribund flesh . . . the flesh of *those* kind . . . the kind that had kept his old self from succeeding in the old world. The kind that insisted in myriad ways that he didn't have what it took.

This old world invader would not foil his new self. He would not prevent Henri from performing his duties in the name of the New World.

Henri understood: *this* was his final test before he was deemed worthy to proceed out into in the old world in the name of the dragon.

Studying the invader's defensive and offensive methods, narrowing on those colorful crisscross patterns about his body, Henri deciphered what they meant—specifically, what they meant for the invader's defeat.

Henri had what he needed. When he saw his chance, he flexed his wings and dove in.

FIVE

Neal gazed at the dark angels emerging from the burnt-orange clouds. Each was roughly the size of an adult human—but there were no signifiers of gender. Their hides were greenish blue in tone, making them initially appear as flying shadows against the orange vapor. Yet, as they approached, they came into greater definition.

Their bodies were lean and barbed. Their yellow eyes, fierce and blazing. Their wings, sharp-edged and shapeshifting. And their sound . . . a maniacal trilling. They almost seemed like transmogrified starlings as they dove toward him in waves.

They swooped by, scratching at him, attempting to smack or slice him with their wings. Neal spun, dodged, and otherwise evaded as well as he could—but he ensured he touched each and every one that didn't touch him first.

He smacked, punched, and kicked at them. Some tumbled yet quickly recovered to fly a short distance away and double back. Others, though hit, seemed to shrug off the blows as they put farther distance between Neal and themselves before looping back.

He wouldn't unleash any significant firepower until he understood what he was facing. Part of the learning experience was getting knocked around a bit as touching his foes sparked and ignited a telepathic talent that, after repeated grazing, flared up within Neal, telling him their story.

These creatures had been bred to go out into the world, appetize on flesh, and imbibe souls, leaving what's left of the carcasses to amalgamate into workers and servants for some Grand Iniquity, the very monster in which Neal now fought.

After three rounds of attack, the dark angels pulled back, surrounding him. Some hovered high in the air; others levitated just above the ground. From point to point, they were positioned like the vertexes of a dome jungle gym, placing Neal at its center.

Neal rotated, keeping an eye on all while surveying their surroundings for other dangers. He now noticed, of all the dark angels that had emerged from the cloud, all but one had attacked. One had remained aloft, higher than the rest, holding back. Neal figured it was the highest-ranking among them, the on-site commander of the crew who now redoubled their efforts, launching in from every direction.

Neal's defenses were up and ready as they swiped and slashed at him. Some flew by swiftly, attempting to keep him off balance, while others kept in close, their claws attempting to latch on and play with his body like clay.

The fliers landed their blows as well, smacking and swatting at him with their wings. When connecting, the wings left a residue that rapidly attracted swarms of tiny pests, like flies to sugar—a clinging mass Neal couldn't swat away.

As the swarms grew, the dark angels pulled back to their

positions on the invisible dome. The miniscule pests were the second line of attack; their methods, more psychological.

Neal writhed in a cloud of tiny dark angels, thousands of them, vengeful and combative, too tiny and too quick to be touched, while they danced with his unwilling senses.

As he spun and twisted—attempting to bat them away while also trying to get a read on their purpose and weaknesses—he winded up only touching himself, striking at himself, pretzeling his telepathic ability, stirring inadvertent and painful memories.

*If only I'd been stronger. If only—*

*No.* He wouldn't retreat back to his past. He wouldn't dwell. No passive regression.

Though he couldn't figure what might be anathema to the minute angels, he had read the bigger ones. And as he focused on them, ignoring the tiny pests, he saw they'd retained their formation. They were on the verge of swooping in to deliver their final blows; yet they were also sweetly positioned for him to draw a new constellation.

He managed to tag each of them only once before they flexed their wings and dove in. It was enough. Having already read them, he needed only to recall their signatures and tighten the connections. Their swiftness forced him to do so quickly.

His resultant barrage was necessarily less refined than before—rather than carve, he was forced to paint with large doses of radiation—but it was no less effective.

Unfortunately, it may have been more than enough.

The incoming dark angels shrilled as the liquid-light coursing through them vomited out of their bodies' rapidly multiplying orifices, *churging* out as polychromatic sludge while what remained of their skins turned gray; whatever bony structures were inside became friable; and the would-be harbingers of a new world disintegrated into dust.

Neal stumbled and collapsed, exhausted. He'd given more than he should have. But he wasn't finished. Not yet.

Trembling, he heaved himself up to his knees. It took another strained effort to raise his chin, lifting his gaze from the ashes toward the heart as he wondered if he had just enough left to stop it.

His eyes met the remaining dark angel, the one who'd held back, now coming in faster than he could trace.

Neal struggled to throw up a quick-and-dirty force field —but the dark one passed through it like water through sieve.

The dark one crashed into Neal, embracing him like a long-lost sibling—a mad brother who'd returned from a world away to reclaim a stolen inheritance. Such was Neal's impression as the angel's barbs pierced his skin. Neal unleashed a scream that sounded as if it had been kept prisoner for years within the deepest pit inside him.

Bypassing Neal's reflexive defenses, the dark angel's prickles injected some equivalent of poison that forced his insides to throb with a jagged rhythm. Neal's screaming seemed to fall in line with the rhythm as the two remained locked in embrace, spinning like spiteful dancers, while Neal's thoughts became blindingly vivid.

He realized the creature was reading his mind, scrambling what it read, and then feeding the bad thoughts—the worst memories—back to Neal so that he saw them all as a tortuous mosaic.

*Violations . . . the searing violations of body, mind . . . and soul . . .*

Neal writhed fiercely, fighting back with enough force

to push them to the ground. The dark one didn't loosen its grip.

Rolling in ashes, Neal felt his body leaking, losing its essence. He struggled to ignore his pain, focusing deeper within himself, consciously striving to access his entire arsenal of tactics, defensive and offensive.

His body spasmed as his telepathic sense kicked up and flared. Reading the dark angel's mind, he learned just enough about the twisted soul, some assorted facts of its pre-downcycled history.

A selection of black patches on Neal's soul-skin inhaled deeply, tugging at the dark angel's body, ripping away and subsuming miniscule snatches, chewing on them, analyzing them.

As if suddenly feeling the danger to itself, the dark angel shoved away from Neal, flexing its wings to lift itself off the ground.

Neal remained lying on his back. He made no attempt to sit up, let alone stand. His tired eyes met the angel's as it hovered nearby.

They shared a sense of mutual appreciation. It wasn't respect but something more akin to pity.

Arches of faint light rose from Neal's body as the white patches of his soul-skin brightened, became increasingly luminous. Seeing the flickers about his abdomen, he now struggled to get to his feet, baiting the dark angel with gestures as he did.

The dark angel remained where it was, keeping Neal in its sights. It had a do-or-die mission to accomplish as well. But it seemed hesitant.

Standing, Neal's body pulsated, flashing like a warning. The dark angel was perhaps figuring how to end Neal without having to touch him.

Neal was perfectly happy for the angel to remain where it was so that he could release what had been pent up, what he could no longer contain, directing it all toward the angel in such an intense yet broad swath that even if it tried to dart away—as it did, in a hurried flutter—it wouldn't escape.

The dark angel had likely known that Neal was cooking up something repellant. What the angel couldn't have known is that the bits and pieces of him that had been consumed by Neal's body would be converted and expelled as extremely poisonous radiation—deadly for the target who'd been partially eaten.

The dark angel did not disintegrate like the others. Nor did it make any sound as its body melted and *sploshed* to the ground, forming an amber puddle cradled by the ashes of its fellows.

Neal's entire frame wobbled. His body continued to leak from the puncture wounds—wounds that would not be healed.

The wounded body of an Artzman . . . He was unstable. He wouldn't last much longer.

He mustered what strength he could for a mad dash toward the heart. Nearing it, the gaseous cloud dissipated, giving him the clearest view yet of the massive, rotating structure before him: a triple helix of twizzling maroon ropes. What had simply been bright ovoids before now seemed like giant eggs displaying a wild variety of colorful designs. The oval objects were embedded in the rope's grooves, running the entire length. The portion Neal saw was at least half a mile long—more than enough for him to work with.

When within a sufficient distance, he leaped and forced his psychokinetic talents to lift and propel him as far as it could into the heart, deep enough for him to latch on to and maintain a firm grip on one of the cords.

*. . . clinging for dear half-life.*

*A joke. What a joke.*

The mind did weird things when it understood its vessel was near death. Neal climbed for the nearest orb, scaling at the speed of an athlete who'd unwisely come out of retirement. He had to pause, frequently, giving the beast its last-ditch efforts to strike at his mind.

*. . . failure . . . failure . . . failure . . .*

Neal countered the dreadful rhythm by focusing on his first compassionate encounter with Valentinus. When accepting the offer to give up his humanity for a greater Gift, Neal also accepted some words of wisdom from the archangel: "Love is not about sex. Or friendship. Or companionship. It goes deeper. It's about *Creation.*"

Neal remembered that message now as he reached an orb. He let the dazzling egg blind him as he focused, concentrating what was left of his ability to project narrow force fields to jackhammer at the shell.

Once sufficiently cracked, he crawled inside, penetrating the gooey liquid-light that had been encased, protected no longer.

Like a sentient blob able to morph into substances hard and soft, the liquid-light assaulted his body. Though he barely moved, he experienced the sensations of sliding down, ascending and whirling, corkscrewing, bending in impossible ways, and being tied into a series of knots. He'd expected this and more—and didn't care. His vessel had outlived its usefulness. Whatever and whomever could fight and play with it till content.

Neal worked his mind and what was left of his soul by concentrating on crisscrossing patterns, vibrating outward.

His body was pierced, lacerated. Searing flames streaked through forgotten muscles and cords. What felt like a sour stomach became an expanding quicksand for physical sensations and what remained of his human emotions.

But he had left the body. His mind was one with his soul, manifesting now as two strings of black-and-white beads, two chains that coiled around one another as they broke free of the orb, grew and expanded, becoming entwined with the twisting cords of the beast's heart.

Neal imparted secret knowledge to the creature, not through words, but a code—a tangible static that smoothed into a visual melody, a brilliant and beautiful song about streets paved in gold, gates of pearl . . .

Neal's very essence dissipated in wisps of various hues as he felt the impetus within the beast dissolving, its form metamorphosing into a site of peace and beauty.

The dying colossal beast was transforming into a city resting on several hills, a metropolis of jasper, pearl, and gold, crystal and jewels, smoldering with incense. It was a city of impossible streets, alleys, buildings, and other structures navigable only by those of reworked bodies, elevated souls.

The gleaming, sprawling structure could comfortably house hundreds of thousands. But would not do so in this place and time.

For now, Neal sensed Valentinus—with the assistance of others—working to cordon off the land on which the defeated Arigrian lay, making it invisible to all living eyes and undetectable by any humanmade sensors. The archangel passed him a final thank-you, with a promise to create a slice of a space-time—a bubble within stained glass —where the city would reside until the End of History.

Neal didn't bother to hope for resurrection. His life cycle was complete. He'd come out of darkness to slay a dragon from hell, turning it into a gift for the Hereafter, a gift to the remnants of humankind.

# SIX

Henri lay with his compatriots.

Like them, like all within the body of the new-life-giving dragon, he had passed through many states of being. At present he lay as a puddle, a liquefied solid. Recent memories and ruminations shimmered on his surface.

The dissolution of a body after death . . . The potential final division of the soul and the body . . . Pessimistic men and women might imagine there's no fruitful afterlife if one passes from the world without achieving the proper unity between the two—just the right combination that unlocks the entry to one's true purpose in life. Once the breath of life leaves the body—purpose unachieved—the body disintegrates, the breath evaporates. A wasted life. The human run ends in oblivion.

But he wasn't human. He was part of the New World. And he wasn't waste. None who had been chosen and saved by the dragon were. They were participants in a grand sacrifice—the unified sacrifice of themselves and their maker.

And their work wasn't done.

As his remains and those of his compatriots mixed, a vapor arose, passing them into their next phase.

They'd transcended their bodies, and they'd transcend the husk of the dragon. They'd transcend many barriers.

They'd let themselves be carried with the winds, the ever-influential winds, hoping that what they stood for, what they sought to achieve might inspire the still-human, the deep-breathing, the ambitious.

SEVEN



*The mourning after . . .*

The air reeked of stinkweed and corpse flowers—a bouquet comparatively sweeter to Remy than what he'd inhaled yesterday.

He'd declined to travel back to Texas, insisting on staying in Oklahoma. He further insisted that his debriefing take place on the site of the *Outflow*, reasoning that it was important for understanding what their next battles might entail, and how they might win them.

Today as yesterday, he remained "the man." The man who'd gone charging into the snarling face of danger. The highest-ranking man on the ground under whose leadership they'd managed to eke out a victory. The man who was damned lucky to have some beyond-space-and-time assistance.

His future achievements would rely far less on luck.

First, his human allies had some lessons to learn.

Riding high on the respect and admiration he momentarily commanded, he called for his immediate superiors and everyone under his command to be present—a good-size portion of the "spectral forces"—for a mass debriefing that he staged as a rally.

The women and men were arrayed before him as he spoke near the very site where his mobile command unit sat when the beast underwent its final transformation.

The unit remained in place. The transformed beast and a significant portion of the land on which it had rested was gone from sight. And though the features of the landscape were markedly different, any innocent passing through would see no sign of what had transpired.

One had to know how to look.

There were still traces of electrical activity in the air—occasional crackles, whiffs of something burning, and subtle vibrations partially obscured by the gentle breezes.

None of it was likely noticed by anyone other than Remy as he harangued the tidy crowd, relaying what he'd seen, what he'd heard, and what he'd learned the previous day.

When he thought them sufficiently enthralled by his experience, he paused to take a long, studied breath—as did the mesmerized women and men, following his lead.

The air had shifted. Notes of cardamom, ginger, and cinnamon filled their nostrils as the breezes wafted hints of the ultimate plan, providing subtext to everything Remy had been relating while transmitting ideas as to how they might proceed in working toward the ideal state of Creation.

When the command came for them to undress, none hesitated to obey.

Their clothes folded neatly and stacked in a pile next to where they stood, naked, the women and men arrayed before Remy directed their attention toward where he gestured and followed his lead into further breathing exercises.

The rally became a baptism by mingled air as, with strengthening telepathic links, the women and men of the spectral forces shared the experience of transformation, accumulating particulates and information from the atmosphere.

Their skin itched all over, as if the loose strings of a body-size net lay on them, slowly becoming more taunt. None of them dared to scratch, even as the imagined net tightened, squeezing their now-tingling skin as it sank deeper, under the skin, which felt as if electric currents were passing through it.

They sensed a hum coming from deep within their brains. As its intensity grew, their eyes stuttered in their sockets, throwing their vision into disarray.

None of them moved a step. None uttered a sound. All tasted hints of metal, as if they were tasting an aspect of the grid that was fusing their senses, altering their bodies.

Their muscles twitched. The consistency of their blood changed—spurting through their arteries, churging through their veins—as their hearts followed the rapid rhythm of ballooning out like grapes and withering into raisins.

While their innards roiled, inches-long filaments sprouted from their skin and trilled as the breezes ran through them.

The congregants' eyes settled in their sockets, introducing them to a new type of vision.

They could now see through the stained veils. They could see the city clearly. They could communicate with its ghosts.

They could now carry on in the name of the dragon.

With shut eyes and controlled breathing, their forms

reverted to bodies that were human in appearance only. They got dressed in a mechanical fashion and gradually dispersed, heading home to await the next call to action.

Remy remained where he stood, gazing into nothing as his vision blurred and his thoughts sharpened.

He was still the duty-bound man. The struck-lucky man . . . The one who, the day before, had gotten his first whiff of things to come and had acted accordingly to be a part of it.

The urge to protect, to defend, to perform service in the preservation of an idea, pushing toward the establishment of the ideal, had not died within him. It had only become stronger. The same urge would be instilled and grow within others.

The necessary change in the human species was underway. He and the spectral forces would be the vanguard, working in service of the *ideal* of what the species should become. A large number of the present-day humans were unnecessary to the end goal, but they could be repurposed. That was justice. Divine fairness. Everyone would have a glorious purpose, even if it was simply as fuel.

Remy was no longer clueless.

A man *could* change his nature.

He could be reborn to help reshape the state of Creation.

# ABOUT THE SERIES

When their bodies are overwhelmed by an onslaught of parasites that feed on blood and light, most victims of the White Fire Virus die quickly but in excruciating pain. They could be considered the lucky ones. Those who survive continue to live on in physical and psychological torment; they also find themselves endowed with a range of supernatural abilities. Many of these survivors consider themselves angels, potential saviors of humanity. Others want nothing less than the death of God. And there are a few who are even more ambitious.

Eve of Light is a dark metaphysical fantasy—philosophical, intense, action-packed, and *surreal*.

## The Core Novels

*BloodLight: The Apocalypse of Robert Goldner*
*Broken Angels* (Eve of Light, Book I)
*Divinities, Entangled* (Eve of Light, Book II)

## The Deviant-Hunter Stories

*Deviant-Hunter: Blood Oath*
*Deviant-Hunter, Killer of Saints*
*Deviant-Hunter's Sabbath*

## Other Stories on the Fringe

*The Lark*

*Heaven's Gun*
*Rogue Beauty*
*FoolKillers*
*Knotty & Ice*
*Influx*

# EVE OF LIGHT STORY ORDER

Although it is recommended that readers begin the series with either a standalone story or *Broken Angels*, there is no suggested reading order. What follows, however, is a list of where the current stories generally fall within the timeline of events.

*The Lark*
*BloodLight: The Apocalypse of Robert Goldner*
*Heaven's Gun*
*Rogue Beauty*
*Deviant-Hunter: Blood Oath*
*Deviant-Hunter, Killer of Saints*
*Deviant-Hunter's Sabbath*
*Broken Angels* (Eve of Light, Book I)
*FoolKillers*
*Knotty & Ice*
*Divinities, Entangled* (Eve of Light, Book II)
*Influx*

# ABOUT THE AUTHOR

Harambee K. Grey-Sun is the author of several novels, novellas, and short stories, including *Hero Zero, Colder Than Ice,* and *Unfair Play.* For more information about his books and ongoing projects, please visit www.harambee-greysun.com.

*For more information:*

Click Here for Author's Website
www.harambeegreysun.com

# ALSO BY HARAMBEE K. GREY-SUN

Standalone Stories

Beholder

Love Among the Ultramoderns

Unfair Play

Last Contact

The Lure

Colder Than Ice

The *HERO ZERO* Series

Hero Zero

BY HARAMBEE GREY-SUN

<u>Poetry</u>

Spring's Fall (Autumn Numbers * Book I)

Wine Songs, Vinegar Verses

Trinity & Its Twin